THIS WRETCHED SPLENDOUR

a play in two acts by Rebecca Wilby

SKYLIGHT PRESS

Performing Rights

All rights whatsoever in this play are strictly reserved. Amateurs and professionals considering a production must apply to the publisher for consent before starting rehearsal or booking a theatre. **No performance may take place unless a licence has been obtained.**

It is a condition of the licence agreement for productions of *This Wretched Splendour* that no changes whatsoever are made in the text. The author of the play must be credited in all programmes and advertising materials distributed in connection with performances of the play.

Applications for performance by professionals and non-professionals throughout the world should be addressed to the Performing Rights Manager, Skylight Press, 210 Brooklyn Road, Cheltenham, GL51 8EA, England. Applications can also be made via the publisher's website: *www.skylightpress.co.uk*

This Wretched Splendour opened at the Playhouse Theatre in Cheltenham on 6th September 1997, with the following cast:

2nd Lieutenant David Cartwright	David Singer
Sergeant Bobby Ashford	Tony Maisey
Corporal Peter Ingham	Peter Young
Lance-Corporal Conor O'Dell	Simon Morgan
Private Sammy Doyle	Nick Mazonowicz
Private Clem Lawrence	Stuart Berrisford
Private Arthur Burrows	Gareth Lomas

Directed by David Wheeler
Set design by Carol Meredith
Lighting by Adrian Hensley
Stage Manager Geoff Marshall

Presented by the Playhouse Company

The first London production of *This Wretched Splendour* was presented by Richard Jackson for Jay Productions at the Grace Theatre in Battersea on 10th February 1998, with the following cast:

2nd Lieutenant David Cartwright	Danny Swanson
Sergeant Bobby Ashford	Gerard Casey
Corporal Peter Ingham	Phil Jervis
Lance-Corporal Conor O'Dell	Stephen Armstrong
Private Sammy Doyle	Max Wrottesley
Private Clem Lawrence	Robert Laughlin
Private Jerry Turner	Glyn William Owen
Private Arthur Burrows	Glenn Hanning

Directed by Ninon Jerome
Designed by Timothy Meaker
Lighting by Jason Larcombe

Produced by Richard Jackson

Left to right: Stuart Berrisford as Clem, Nick Mazonowicz as Sammy, and Tony Maisey as Bobby.

Playhouse Theatre, Cheltenham, 1997.

Left to right: Tony Maisey as Bobby, Nick Mazonowicz as Sammy, and Gareth Lomas as Arthur.

Playhouse Theatre, Cheltenham, 1997.

Photographs by Rebecca Wilby.

CHARACTERS

2nd Lieutenant David Cartwright

Sergeant Bobby Ashford

Corporal Peter Ingham

Lance-Corporal Conor O'Dell

Private Sammy Doyle

Private Clem Lawrence

Private Jerry Turner

Private Arthur Burrows

The action of the play takes place in a British front line trench in the Ypres Salient in the autumn of 1916.

SONGS

If You Want the Sergeant Major (p.24) – traditional soldiers' song

Lloyd George, Lloyd George (p.27) – parody of Baa Baa Black Sheep written by an unidentified soldier of the Gloucestershire Regiment, c.1916

Van Roogy (p.34) – words by Russell Thompson and Rebecca Wilby (roughly fits the tune of 'Molly Malone' or 'Hares on the Mountain', but any tuneless wailing will do)

Tipperary (p.55) – parody lyrics by Private Wilfred Bouch, Canadian Expeditionary Force (killed at Ypres, April 1915)

'We're here because we're here' (p.58) is sung to the tune of Auld Lang Syne

Abide With Me (p.78) – words by H.F. Lyte, music by W.H. Monk

For the opening of Act Two, John McCormack's 1919 recording of **Roses of Picardy** is recommended.

ACT ONE, SCENE ONE

*Ypres, 1916. A British trench in the front line. At back is a high embankment of earth held together with wood and wire, cluttered with bits of debris – shell fragments, spent bullets, splinters of ammunition boxes, etc. The top is lined with a double layer of sand-bags, above which can be seen a few curling fragments of barbed wire. Beyond this is a grey sky tinged with red. The bank has a fire-step on which a soldier slouches with his rifle only half poised, his back to the audience. It is **Clem Lawrence**. Further along the step **Arthur Burrows** and **Jerry Turner** sit side by side sharing a magazine; neither shows much interest in it. Further still along the step the 'youngster' of the platoon, **Sammy Doyle,** is lying stretched out asleep under a thin blanket; all that can be seen of him is a tin hat at one end and a pair of boots at the other. Centre stage are two ammunition crates. **Conor O'Dell,** an Irishman, sits on one writing a letter with a short stub of pencil, using a mess-tin on his lap to lean on. He has a single stripe on the sleeve of his tunic, and a set of rosary beads dangling round his neck, and he crouches over his letter with a frown of concentration. On the other crate sits **Peter Ingham**, whose sleeve bears two stripes, reading an English newspaper. There is an air of despondency and boredom over the whole scene. **Peter** sighs, tuts and grunts disapprovingly as he reads, crossing and uncrossing his legs each time.*

Peter Another cock-up down the other end of the line, by the look of it.

*Nobody takes any notice of him. He glances at **Conor** but he is engrossed in his letter and doesn't look up.*

Peter I don't know, we make an advance on the Boche and half our boys get splatted, and then as soon as we've mopped up their trenches they all come back and splat the other half and we're back where we started, except we've got no men left.

Conor looks up momentarily with an irritated frown, and goes back to his writing.

Peter It's just bloody slaughter. Look at the length of the bloody Casualty List!

*He opens out the newspaper and pushes it in front of **Conor's** face. **Conor** doesn't look at it.*

Peter I don't see how anybody's ever going to win the war if all we keep doing is running backwards and forwards pinching their trenches and then having them pinched straight back again.

Conor	Shut up, will you?
Peter	No, you shut up. Four days of solid fighting, it says here, and we hardly gained a scrap of land. Our lads didn't even stand a chance.
Conor	*(impatiently)* I'm trying to write a letter.
Peter	Oh, that's right, just forget about it and get on with the important things in life. Don't you want to know what's happening on the rest of the front?
Conor	Not if it's junked up nonsense from an English bloody paper. An out-of-date English paper.
Peter	Well where else are we supposed to find out news? Fat chance of anyone out here telling us anything.
Conor	I seen quite enough of the war for meself, thank you very much.

Peter makes a contemptuous noise and goes back to his newspaper. Conor continues with his letter. There is a pause during which Peter turns over the page. A moment later he leaps up with a shout, startling the others.

Peter	Oh! Look at this, look at this! There's been a zeppelin shot down by two British cruisers and a submarine, off the German coast! There's a picture of it here, look. On May 4th. *(disappointed)* Blimey, that was ages ago.
Conor	*(throwing down his pencil)* Look, I couldn't care less if they'd shot down a hundred zeppelins off the coast of Timbuktu, I'm fed up with being here, there's hardly any of us left, the whole thing's a total bloody mess, I don't want to know, and I'm writing a letter to my sister.
Peter	All right, all right. You want to watch it, I think Fritz is getting to you.
Conor	Ay, and I'll be getting to Fritz in a minute, it might be a bit quieter over there in the Boche trenches.
Peter	That's not the soldierly spirit! Come on fellers, all together now, are we downhearted?
Arthur	Sod off, Peter.

They sit in silence for a moment, resuming their reading and writing. Sammy groans and shifts about restlessly in his sleep.

Peter	*(to Sammy)* Christ, don't you start.
Conor	Leave the boy alone, he's been up all night on sentry duty. He's due for a bit of kip.

Peter	Hey, Clem. Conor wants to know whether it's quieter in the Boche trenches than here.
Clem	Well I don't know, I haven't been taking any notice. I'm having a game here. *(he shows a pack of playing cards that he has been concealing in front of him)*
Peter	You'll get shot.
Clem	Nah. There aren't any officers here to catch me on this side, and there certainly aren't any Germans bothering to shoot at me from that side. More likely to die of boredom at this rate.
Jerry	Don't knock it.
Peter	Yeah, there'll be time enough for dodging bullets when the Kaiser gets his act together.
Clem	And plenty of time to finish this game before then, I reckon.
Peter	It's all happening down at the French end by the look of it. *(he taps his newspaper)*
Clem	Well isn't this France?
Peter	Um... no, I think it's Belgium.
Clem	Well, I was told when I came out here that I was going to France.
Peter	I think we're quite near France. Oi, Conor, is this France or Belgium?
Conor	I don't know. France, I think.
Clem	There you go.
Peter	Well, I know we're by a place called Wipers. Isn't that in Belgium?
Jerry	You don't say Wipers, it's supposed to be – *(he pauses to summon up an affected accent)* Eepra.
Clem	Eepra. That sounds French to me.
Peter	All right then, next time I get a chance to go into the town I'll ask someone, is this France or Belgium.
Clem	How will you ask them when you don't know whether to speak to them in French or Belgiumese?
Jerry	There's no such language as Belgiumese.
Clem	So what do they speak in Belgium then?
Jerry	French.
Clem	Well Peter doesn't speak French anyway.
Peter	Neither does anybody else.

Clem   Do you speak Belgiumese, Peter?

Peter   I thought you said there was no such language?

Clem   I didn't say that.

Jerry   No, I did.

Peter   Do you speak it then?

Jerry   No, I don't speak anything.

Clem   And neither does anybody else.

Conor   So what are you all arguing about it for?

A thoughtful silence ensues.

Arthur   Does anybody speak German?

Peter   What kind of a question is that?

Clem   You could run across and ask one of the fellers over the other side of the field, they might help.

Arthur   No, no, I'm serious. Does anybody here speak it?

Clem   You heard what we were just saying. Nobody here speaks anything.

Peter   Not even English in Clem's case.

Clem blows a raspberry.

Arthur   Well I've got this diary, see. I think it's a diary anyway.

Peter   Cor, wow, let's have a look.

Clem   *(coming down from the firestep)* Yeah, come on Arthur, let's see it.

Peter   You can't come down here, Clem Lawrence, you're supposed to be keeping an eye on the Boche.

Clem   Bugger the Boche.

Arthur rummages in his pockets and takes out a small leather-bound book. Everybody crowds round, including Conor, his letter temporarily abandoned.

Peter   What does it say?

Arthur   I don't know.

Clem   *(disappointed)* It's all in German.

Jerry   Where did you get it from, Arthur?

Arthur   I found it.

Peter   Well we'd gathered that.

Jerry   Did you pinch it from a Hun?

Arthur   He was dead.

Peter	The best sort.
Arthur	He was lying on the steps of a dug-out after we'd bombed them out. I wanted some kind of souvenir to send my mum, so I had a look in his pockets.
Peter	Was there anything else on him? Pictures of the Kaiser buggering a dachshund?
Clem	Chains and leather whips and stuff?
Arthur	No, there was just this, with a photograph inside it of a woman and a little girl. I sent the photograph to my mum. Didn't think she'd want the book, what with it being all in German and that.
Clem	Go on Jerry, you read it out.
Jerry	Oh, err, I'll have a go. *(reading slowly and awkwardly)* "Free-tagg nine-sten Joony nineteen-sixteen." Oh well, that looks like the date, doesn't it? "Meen arbeet ist geggen mittag zoo end." I wonder what a zoo end is?
Clem	Sounds like some kind of gun.
Arthur	Yeah, mortar-firer or something. Bastards.
Jerry	"Dan war itch mud…" or is it "muddy"?
Arthur	Well that's obviously talking about war and mud, isn't it? What are those little blobs over the 'u'?
Clem	Leaky pen I expect.
Jerry	"… weel itch die ganzy zeet ste-hen" something.

Sammy begins to thrash around in his sleep, groaning and trying to turn over in sporadic, jerky movements.

Peter	Hey up, you're giving Sammy nightmares.
Jerry	"Abber um soll-dat zoo werden…"
Arthur	What's that? A zoo warden?
Peter	Surely not…

Sammy makes a fierce attempt to turn over and wrap the blanket around himself at the same time, and in doing so rolls off the firestep and crashes to the floor. Nobody takes any notice of him and he doesn't wake up.

Jerry	"… soll man orf-merk-sam, selb-standig und muttig seen."
Clem	Very good, Jerry, but what does it mean?
Jerry	Well…
Peter	Shit! Sarge's coming!
Clem	Holy Christ.

*Clem leaps up onto the firestep and assumes an alert, vigilant position, his rifle poised on the parapet. **Arthur** puts away the diary. A moment later **Bobby** enters. He is a sergeant, young and bright-looking, and it is clear that the others respect him.*

Bobby   Right, stand to, I've got some news for you. And you, Clem. We haven't had any Germans come out of their trenches in the last three weeks, so you might as well come down off there for a minute.

Arthur   Well, this sounds exciting, doesn't it?

Jerry   *(shaking **Sammy**, who is still lying on the floor, wrapped cocoon-like in his blanket)* Come on Sam, wakey wakey.

Sammy   What's happening?

Jerry   Don't know. Sarge's going to tell us something.

Sammy   Is the war over?

Jerry   It might as well be. Not that anybody would bother to tell us about it.

Bobby   Yes, well it's what we're going to do if it livens up a bit that worries me. I've just been down to company HQ and Major Ramsbotham says we can't have any more men for the moment.

Peter   What?

Conor   But we're down to a fraction of our strength.

Bobby   That's just too bad. Apparently they're still short of men after the big push down in France. They had a lot more casualties than they thought. And it seems they're still hard at it with what they've got left, so all the new drafts coming over from England are being sent straight into the line down there, and they can't spare any.

Jerry   Bloody great.

Conor   What happens if we have another show up here?

Bobby   Um… well, we all get killed, basically. But the idea is that the Germans won't attack us up here while they're being kept under pressure down in Picardy.

Clem   Oh. Well that's nice. How thoughtful of them.

Conor   But look. They had one of the worst battles up here in – when was it? End of '14. Then six months later it happened again, even worse. Surely to God those in-bred crustaceans up in high command don't think the Kaiser's given up on this place? He'll be down on us like a ton of bricks just when we don't expect it.

14

Peter	That's right Conor, you tell 'em. We'll make a general of you yet.
Sammy	He's right though. The higher the rank the fewer the brains.
Bobby	Hang on, hang on, there's more. With typical army organisation and logical planning they are sending us a new officer.

There is a general murmur of disapproval.

Peter	We don't want an officer. What's the point in having an officer in charge of – (*he pauses to check the number of his companions*) seven men?
Bobby	I think the idea is that we have somebody in charge ready for when they do have some troops going spare and can send us a new draft.
Clem	Oh, that's great that is. I wonder how many platoons there are with no officers left, and here we are with an officer and no bleeding platoon.
Sammy	Is he going to be like the last one?
Peter	They're all the same.
Clem	They're not sending us Major Ramsbotham are they?
Bobby	God no. He wouldn't come within half a mile of the front line in case he got shit all over his boots.
Arthur	So when is this chap coming?
Bobby	He's here.
Sammy	(*looking round*) What?
Bobby	No, not *here* here. He's down at HQ talking to the major.
Peter	You've seen him?
Bobby	Only through the window.
Peter	What's he like?
Bobby	I don't know. Like an officer I suppose. Walking-stick and silly trousers.
Peter	And what's his name?
Bobby	(*taking a crumpled bit of paper from his pocket and consulting it*) Second-Lieutenant D. Cartwright.
Jerry	Second-Lieutenant, eh? He can't have been out here long then. All the second-lieutenants I've ever known have got themselves shot within six months.
Clem	Or packed off home with a blighty.
Arthur	God, I hope it's not the last one we had, sent back out here again.

Peter	He wasn't called Cartwright.
Arthur	No, but he might be using a false name. I think I would if I had his track record.
Clem	Yes, he brought new meaning to the word 'funk', didn't he? I mean it's fair enough to shoot yourself in the foot if you want to get sent home, but to drink a bottle of Worcester sauce... it's not very sportsmanlike, is it?
Jerry	He should have been court-martialled.
Sammy	The Worcester sauce was nothing. You should have tried sharing a dug-out with him. He used to –
Bobby	It's all right chaps, I can promise you this one is not the same bloke. If it is I will personally shoot him to save him the embarrassment of having to poison himself.
Clem	Sarge?
Bobby	What?
Clem	Is this France or Belgium?
Bobby	*(after a moment's pause)* It's Flanders.
Clem	You don't know, do you?
Bobby	Now just you watch your lip –
Sammy	Do you really think there's going to be another big show up here? Is that why they're sending us an officer?
Bobby	There's always going to be heavy fighting in a place like this, Sammy, because it's a salient. If they let us retreat just to the other side of Wipers it wouldn't be half so bad.
Jerry	You don't say Wipers, you say Eepra.
Sammy	What's a salient?
Bobby	Rubbish. Even the generals call it Wipers.
Sammy	People are always talking about the salient but nobody ever says what it is.
Peter	It's a sticky-outy bit.
Bobby	It's an area that juts out into enemy territory so –
Peter	*(interrupting indignantly)* That's what I said.
Bobby	– so you're surrounded by the enemy on three sides and it's three times as difficult to defend it. This one is particularly bad because the Germans are on higher ground than us. They can even chuck shells to the rear of our position with their big guns. They're

	going to take this place one day and they know it. They're just biding their time.
Sammy	Oh right. I wondered why it always seems like the whizz-bangs are coming from every direction at once. I thought it was just my imagination.
Clem	I don't reckon they are biding their time over there. I reckon they've all gone home. No, seriously. When was the last time any of you saw a Hun? I've been standing up there all day and haven't seen hide nor hair of them. How about you, Sammy, did you see anyone when you were on the watch last night?
Sammy	No, not a sausage.
Clem	There you are then. I bet those trenches over there are all empty and they're having a great laugh watching us all standing around here like a bunch of bleeding idiots.
Jerry	They're still shelling us.
Clem	Yes but only a bit. They've probably just got a couple of artillery chaps to stay behind and chuck the odd five-nine at us every now and then to make it convincing, but we haven't had a single shot fired on us by their infantry in – what? – three weeks?
Arthur	It's a good point actually, it's happened before. That's what the Anzacs did to the Turks last year at Gally-polly. I read about it in the papers.
Bobby	All right then Clem, if you're so sure there are no Germans over there, why don't you take a stroll across No Man's Land and have a look?
Peter	We'll just stand here and watch.
Clem	Ah… well now… it's only an idea. I'm not suggesting –
Bobby	Attention! Fall in, fall in! Get in line there, quick!

*Everybody scrambles into line as quickly as possible and stands rigidly to attention. A moment later **David Cartwright** enters. He is a young officer aged about 24, immaculately turned out with a highly polished Sam Browne belt and cavalry breeches; his sleeve bears a single pip. He is a man of exceptional charisma and his manner is always jolly and easy-going, yet underneath this charm he is also mature, intelligent and caring. As he enters he is cheerfully whistling a popular tune, and strolls towards the line of men at a leisurely pace and with the tiniest trace of a limp, swinging a walking cane rather ostentatiously. **Bobby** salutes.*

Bobby   Sir. 10658 Sergeant Ashford, sir.

Peter   13746 Corporal Ingham, sir.

Conor   14208 Lance-corporal O'Dell, sir.

Sammy   11471 Private Doyle, sir.

Jerry   18945 Private Turner, sir.

Clem   19337 Private Lawrence... *(he tails off)*

David, still whistling pleasantly to himself, has walked straight past them and gone out the other side.

Clem   What's going on? Is he our officer or not?

Bobby   Stand to and shut up.

They stand silently in line for a few moments. After a while Sammy starts to lean forward surreptitiously and look sideways, trying to see where David has gone without moving from his position in the line. He leans at an ever more ridiculous angle until Bobby leans across and jabs him with the end of his rifle.

Bobby   Pack that in.

Sammy   He's gone.

Bobby   I don't care. You stand in line until I tell you otherwise.

They stand in silence again, and begin to shuffle and cough. David strolls quietly in again from behind, where the men can neither see him nor hear him. He stands behind them with a smile on his face.

Sammy   I've got pins and needles.

Bobby   I'll give you a bayonet up your bleeding arse to go with it if you don't shut up.

David   *(startling them all)* Second-lieutenant Cartwright.

Bobby   *(hastily saluting)* Sir.

David   Right, stand at ease, that's got the formalities over with. Now we can get down to biz. I'm David. *(he holds out his hand to Bobby, who hesitates nervously before taking it – partly for the sake of decorum, partly because he doesn't know what to do with his rifle)* And you are...?

Bobby   Ashford, sir. 10658 Sergeant Ashford.

David   Now let's dispense with all that rot. What's your real name?

Bobby   *(reluctantly)* I'm called Bobby, sir.

David   Good, that's more like it. You're the chap who's been running things down here, aren't you?

Bobby	Yes sir, I've been commanding the platoon since our last officer became a casualty, sir.
David	Yes, I heard about that. I don't know, these blasted officers just drop down like flies, don't they? Waste of bally space. *(to Peter)* Now what's your name?
Peter	Peter Ingham, sir.
David	Peter. Jolly good. We'll drop the 'sir' bit though if you don't mind, it makes me feel like a schoolteacher. Or a knight. Can't have that. How about you?
Conor	I'm Conor O'Dell.
David	Aha, a Celt, eh? That's what we like to see. There've been some pretty impressive exploits from the Celtic battalions further down the line. Where are you from?
Conor	I'm a Wicklow man, sir.
David	Excellent. And I see you've got your worry beads on you just in case. And you are...?
Sammy	Sam Doyle, sir – I mean not sir.
David	Oh yes, I've heard all about you. You were the batman to the last officer who was out here, weren't you? I've heard glowing reports.
Sammy	Really?
David	Fearless on patrol, the major tells me. Mind you, he is a prize imbecile, that major, so I wouldn't want to put too much faith in his opinions. It's not easy to find reliable and honest servants out here though. The last one I had used to pinch my underwear.
Sammy	That's funny. The last officer I served used to pinch *my* underwear.
David	Excellent, excellent. In that case I'll take you on as my batman. I like your sense of humour and you've reassured me that should the necessity ever arise your underwear is worthy of being pinched by an officer.
Sammy	My mum's sending me out some more socks for my birthday.
David	Wonderful. I've just got two of my aunt's hand-knitted thermal vests. We can do a swap. Now then, what's your name?
Jerry	Jerry Turner, sir.
David	Jerry? That's a rather unfortunate name under the present circumstances.
Jerry	*(curtly)* I can't help that, sir.

David   No, I realise it isn't a court-martial offence. I suppose you two are called Fritz and Boche?

Clem   No sir, Clement Lawrence. But I'm usually just called Clem.

David   Oh well, that's short and sweet. And how about you?

Arthur   Arthur Burrows.

David   Good, that's cleared all that up. Now I'll have to find something for you all to do, won't I? I understand this is a fairly quiet part of the line at the moment.

Bobby   At the moment, sir, yes.

Sammy   *(taking advantage of the informality)* Clem thinks the Germans have all gone home.

David   Well, that's a nice thought isn't it? It'll certainly make life a bit easier for us if they have.

Bobby   We haven't seen much activity from the enemy for some weeks now, sir.

Sammy   But we're all too scared to go over there and find out.

Bobby kicks Sammy's backside with a deftness that can only have come from long practice.

David   I see. Let's have a look then.

David walks to the back of the trench, calmly climbs up on the firestep and up to the top of the parapet. He cups his hands around his mouth and calls out into No Man's Land.

David   Coo-ee, Fritz!

Two distant rifle shots ring out. David instinctively flinches, but is quite unruffled. He turns round and climbs down again at a leisurely pace, dusting off his tunic. The others are horrified.

David   No, I'm afraid we're out of luck. They're just keeping a low profile.

Bobby   I wouldn't try tricks like that too often, sir. It's dangerous to show yourself above the parapet in daylight. Too many good snipers about.

David   Even the best snipers aren't much of a danger at that range. You mustn't worry so much. It's not good for you. Give you a weak heart.

Bobby   I wouldn't want you to become a casualty within ten minutes of your arrival, sir. We've seen quite enough of our officers and men go down already, with all due respect, sir.

David   Now I'd like to get a couple of things straightened out right from the start. Firstly, I'm not 'sir', I'm David. Secondly, I don't want to catch anybody here being unnecessarily despondent. We're all stuck out here in this God-forsaken vermin-infested quagmire surrounded by thousands of men who are trying to kill us, so we might as well make the best of it and try to enjoy ourselves as much as the circumstances permit. Life is cheap these days, so you need to squeeze as much out of it as you can. If I catch anyone not enjoying themselves without a valid excuse then I will have no alternative but to submit them to one of my jokes. And then you'll be sorry. Do I make myself clear?

Bobby   Yes. *(he silently mouths the word 'sir' afterwards)*

David   Jolly good. Now, that major chappie gave me some battalion orders to read out to you. What have I done with them? Ah yes, here we are. *(he takes a folded paper from his breast pocket and reads it out)* "My darling David." Golly, that's a bit informal. "I hope the parcel of chocolate reached you all right. I do worry so about the –" No, hang on a minute, that's a letter from my girl. What did I do with the blasted bit of paper the major gave me? *(he delves into his pocket again)* Don't tell me I used it for – Ah, this looks like it. Yes, here we are. "To be read by all commanding officers…" rhubarb rhubarb, blah, blah. "It has become apparent that certain discipline regulations regarding courtesy to officers are being relaxed by soldiers while on Active service. *This practice must cease forthwith.*" That bit was in italics, by the way.

Sammy   *(in an embarrassingly loud stage whisper)* What's italics?

David   "On meeting an officer, the N.C.O. in charge of a platoon or section must immediately call his men to attention and give the officer a full salute. All men wearing hats must also give a full salute. It is not sufficient to acknowledge the officer with anything less than the correct saluting procedure, even if that officer has already been correctly saluted earlier in the same day; neither is it acceptable for the N.C.O. to salute on behalf of the other men where one or more men are wearing hats. This order is to be observed in all circumstances. Officers must report any failure to comply with the regulation and the offenders will be severely dealt with."

He pauses for a moment to let the men take in what they've heard.

David Pish and tush. *(he slowly tears the order to pieces)* What do they think this is, a blasted comedy act? This sort of stuff is fine on the parade ground in peace-time, but this is a war we're in here, not a game of toy soldiers. You will erase this order from your consciousness. From now on we will establish our own code of conduct based on a combination of practicality and mutual respect – man to man, not ranks to officer. It's not that I'm deriding the importance of military discipline, it's just that we need to apply it in the right way, to make us into good soldiers with intelligence, independence and integrity, and not just a flock of sheep running around in front of a barking dog. So, let's set ourselves a little programme to start us off. Every afternoon when you've finished cleaning your rifles you will report here for drill.

Sammy *(disappointed)* Drill? In the trenches?

David That's right, Sam. First of all we will have a singing drill. You all know how to do that I suppose?

Clem We do sing on the march sometimes, but not usually when we're out here in the line.

David Then you obviously need a bit more practice. After that there will be football drill. There's not a lot of room in here, but I'm sure we'll manage. I was just checking out the dug-outs further along the trench to see whether they'd make suitable goals and I think they might just do the job if we bank them up a bit with sandbags. And finally there will be the occasional trip-into-town-to-stock-up-on-wine drill. Is everybody happy with that?

Bobby Yes. Though I'm not sure that Major Ramsbotham would approve.

David I don't really care very much whether Major Sheepsrear approves or not. It's all very well being a stuffy old codger when you're cooped up in a fortified dug-out all day, but it's rather different out here when you know a shell might land on you at any moment. So let's take our beloved major as an example for our first lesson. As I see it, the key to a good strong morale for a soldier at the front is a healthy disrespect for staff officers and for company commanders who never venture out of the officers' mess at company HQ. Ahem, no names, no pack drill. In my last battalion I had a really good major who went over the top with the rest of the troops, until he was killed while trying to bring in some of the wounded. At the other end of the scale you have Major Sheepsrear, who thinks that wars should be conducted like this.

He puffs out his chest and begins to pace up and down in front of the line of men in a jerky goose-step, twirling his walking cane and tucking it under his arm, then twirling it again and tucking it under the other arm, his face set in an affected military grimace. He speaks in a husky voice with an exaggerated aristocratic accent, and barks out the words.

David   You see, the secret of being a dashed faine company commander is to hev a dashed faine military strut, laike so. You hev to get those bally boot soles raight up – raight up laike this – so those filthy working class oiks in the ranks can see the haigh class stitching and the name plate of your exclusive London cobbler stuck to the bottom. Haw! And the cane hyah hes two functions. One is to lean on at opportune moments to corroborate your peck of fibs abight having a gammy leg and being unfit for active service at the front with all the filthy peasants – ai mean with all our brave boys – and the other function is to swing it arind all over the bally shop – haw! – to show the senior officers that one is a dashed gellant chep and all rind good egg and rairly ought to be recommended for an M.C. in recognition of all the jolly heroic exploits that one *would* be getting up to if one were ectually ite at the front. Hwah! Neturally one hes to cultivate the raight kaind of facial expression to make oneself worthy of the name of Sheepsrear and gain the respect of the little blighters in the ranks, so one hes to screw up one's visage, laike so, until it looks not so much laike a human face as a sheep's beck end. And then you spite ite a lot of bally ovine ordure instead of normal comprehensible human speech, thus:

He roars out a drawled command which is totally incomprehensible. The men, joining in the game, all respond with various parade ground movements, but not having understood the command they all do different things. **David** *bellows more nonsensical commands and the men cheerfully respond with a variety of positions until they are in a total muddle and are bumping into each other. Eventually* **Sammy** *drops his rifle, and as he stoops to pick it up* **David** *raps the ground in front of it with the tip of his walking cane.*

David   Haw! Thet mehn there! Wahn pace forward! March!

Sammy steps forward out of the line, stamps and salutes.

Sammy   (*facetiously*) Sir!

David   What do you think you are doing, you uncouth boor?

Sammy   I'm picking up my rifle, sir.

David   No you are not, you are being an uncouth boor. An uncouth boor, demmit!

Sammy   Yes sir.

David   Raifles are not for picking up. They're for waving arind. What would you do if a dirty Hun came running at you raight now, hm?

Sammy   I'd pick up my rifle and shoot him with it, sir.

David   No you would not, you disgusting little mehn. Whai do you think his majesty hes issued all his troops with raifles, hum? Do you think all this expensive equipment is for grubbing arind in the mud and getting the berrel all dirty by shooting filthy Huns? No. It's been proven taime and taime again in bettle situations thet there's nothing the Hun fears more than cold British steel. The bayonet's the thing! There's no bally use in shooting them, thet isn't going to fraighten the dirty beggars is it? They don't hev a blasted chance to be fraightened if they're dead, blast it. Git beck into line. Now you – *(he indicates* **Clem***)* how would you use your raifle in a bettle situation?

Clem   I'd pick it up, wave it arind, and shoot Huns with it, sir.

David   Desh it, mehn! Ebsolute balderdesh! The only way to defeat the Hun is to put the wind up him. You walk boldly forward ite of your trench, sling your raifle on your shoulder with a naice big polished bayonet stuck in the end, and walk straight across No Mehn's Lehnd until you get to the Boche trenches and then you stick your bayonet in the dirty blighters. Cold British steel; it's the only way.

Sammy   What about the Boche machine-guns, sir?

David   Don't be such an ass, mehn. You stick your bayonet in the machine-gunners *first*. Fritz napoo. Compree? Now then, singing drill. And lit's hev something suitably disrespectful. Haw!

Somebody starts singing a version of 'If You Want the Sergeant-Major', and very quickly they have all joined in.

> If you want the sergeant-major, we know where he is,
>
> We know where he is, we know where he is,
>
> If you want the sergeant-major, we know where he is,
>
> He's lying on the canteen floor
>
> We saw him, we saw him,
>
> Lying on the canteen floor
>
> We saw him lying on the canteen floor

If you want to find the colonel, we know where he is,
We know where he is, we know where he is,
If you want to find the colonel, we know where he is,
He's thirty miles behind the line
We saw him, we saw him,
Thirty miles behind the line
We saw him thirty miles behind the line

If you want the old battalion, we know where they are,
We know where they are, we know where they are,
If you want the old battalion, we know where they are,
They're hanging on the barbed wire fence
We saw them, we saw them,
Hanging on the barbed wire fence
We saw them hanging on the barbed wire fence

David *(in his normal voice and manner)* Right, that's enough of that. Stand easy. Now, we're going to have to do something about tarting up this trench just in case Fritz does take it into his head to come and visit us.

Sammy *(nervously)* Have you heard something?

David Yes. Two rifle shots. And I might as well tell you that a few miles up the line they've had some pretty heavy shelling. I don't know that it's coming this way, but it won't do any harm to pile up a few more sandbags on that parapet and check that the wire is all tickety-boo.

Conor There are a couple of small gaps in the wire. I seen them when I was doing sentry duty last week. We caught a German working party out here with their wire-cutters a few weeks ago and opened fire on them, but I think they'd already made a few holes before we spotted them.

Bobby We did report the matter to Major Sheepsr– err, Major Ramsbotham, and asked if we could go out there and fix it up but he said we had to wait until the Royal Engineers sent up a working party.

David   Right. Well I see no Royal Engineers. In that case Conor, you and Arthur can go out tonight as soon as it gets dark and fix up all the gaps you can find, since you know where they are. Better make sure the sentries in the trench next-door know that you're going out so they don't shoot at you. I shall be going out myself later on to have a little recce in No Man's Land; I'd like to get to know the area properly, take a little spin round the estate and see what Uncle Boche is up to. Sam, will you come with me and show me around?

Sammy   Oh yes, I should think I know every tree-stump and shell-hole out there by now.

David   Jolly good. Now, our priority over the next few days is going to be making a couple of nice comfy dug-outs. So I want you all to go scouting around for any useful bits of timber and other materials. After that we will need to stock up on nice things to keep us entertained while we're sitting in the dug-outs, so I'd like Peter and Clem to go and do a bit of shopping.

Peter   *(delighted at the idea)* Can we have a pass to go into Eepra?

David   You don't say Eepra, you say Wipers. But yes, while it's still fairly quiet you may as well go into town and enjoy yourselves, within reason. Here's twenty francs. *(he hands the money to Peter)* Get me some decent local wine, if they have it, and about two dozen chocolate bars, and a large bottle of Worcester sauce.

Peter   *(dubiously)* Right you are.

Clem   Can we get a bottle of van roogy?

David   Get whatever you like, Clem. Only don't drink it all at once. Now, Sam, you can help me shift my baggage up to the dug-out. The rest of you can start filling up a few sandbags. That parapet wants to be a good five feet thick if it's going to be bullet-proof. After that we can have football drill, from which Clem and Peter are excused if they're going into town. We'll have to play three-a-side, but that's about all we've got room for anyway so it doesn't matter much.

Sammy and David go out. The others pick up shovels and empty sandbags and prepare to start work.

Arthur   Nice feller.

Clem   Makes a change.

Jerry   Too clever by half.

Arthur   I wonder if the major knows he's like that?

Bobby   No chance.

Jerry   I hope he means what he says about ignoring the discipline orders. We could all be had up for being insolent to an officer if we're not careful.

Bobby   He seems genuine enough.

Conor   *(ominously)* He'll get killed.

Arthur   Yeah, the good ones always do, don't they?

Peter   Especially if they stick their heads up over the parapet.

Conor   No, I mean it, he'll get killed.

Bobby laughs and slaps him on the shoulder.

Bobby   That's what I like about you, Conor, you're always such a ray of bleeding sunshine, aren't you? Come on you lot, get your backs stuck into it.

Conor shrugs and they begin work, filling the sandbags. They fall into an impromptu rhythm and begin to sing a parody of the nursery rhyme 'Baa Baa Black Sheep'.

> Lloyd George, Lloyd George
>
> Have you any shells?
>
> Yes lads, yes lads,
>
> Guns as well.
>
> Some with high explosive
>
> Others with shrapnel
>
> And some to drop from aeroplanes
>
> And blow the Hun to hell.

ACT ONE, SCENE TWO

The same scene, but at night. The embankment at the back is tidier than before. David sits on an ammunition crate, censoring letters by the light of a small oil-lamp. All is quiet in the trench, but the distant sounds of exploding shells and occasional patter of machine-guns can be heard in the background, and every now and then one sounds a little louder and closer than the rest. The occasional Very light flares in the sky behind.

David *(reading monotonously)* 'I am going on well, though a little fed up with being in the line. Not much chance of getting back to billets at the moment. I got your parcel all right and made short work of Aunt Ethel's fruit cake. Please don't send any more biscuits as there are plenty here but I would like some more cigarettes, Gold Flake if you can get them. Love Peter.' Well, that's a rivetting read.

*He sighs and stamps the letter with the censor's mark. **Conor** and **Arthur** pass by carrying picket stakes and a roll of wire.*

Conor You doing the post?

David Absolutely.

Conor I've another one here for you. *(he hands an envelope to **David**)*

Arthur Me too. *(he hands an envelope to **David**)*

David Thank you. You take care out there tonight, chaps, Fritz is getting a bit skittish by the sound of it.

Arthur Oh, that's nothing. We always get that at night. They drop a few crumps on the chaps down at White-sheet *(he means Wytschaete)*, but they hardly ever bother us here.

Conor We do meet the odd working party out on patrol, but we usually just lob a couple of Mills bombs at them and that keeps them quiet enough.

David Well don't let go of your rifles, just in case.

Arthur Right-o. See you later.

*Conor and **Arthur** go out. **David** opens **Arthur**'s letter with an air of boredom, frowns as he attempts to decipher it, and then brightens up as he begins to read it. It becomes apparent that **Arthur** is not terribly good at spelling, and **David** entertains himself by reading it out phonetically.*

David 'Dearest Mother. I hop you are well. We have not seen any sin of the Botch for a week or two, he must be hiding down in his deep duggets. Our artiggery boys hammer the Botch trenches with whizz-bangs and srapnel bums but I don't reckon it makes no diffyrence if you ask me. When the Botch goes down in his duggets you can't get him out, not with anything. When we had a go at him a copple of weeks ago I went and threw a Mills bum down the steps of a Botch dugget and it only went haff way down becuss there was a bend in the steps and the bum got stuck in it and when it went off it just brote down some dust off the selling and did not kill any Botches.

Toddy we got a new offacer he is called Davvid and I think he is a niece fellow. We played football and had a sing-song and it was quiet good. This is a niece life we have here at the momment I just hop it goes on like this but that depends on this chap Davvid and wither he gets killed like most offacers do. The weather here is niece too and not too muddy. I must go now becuss I do twoddle on too much sometimes.

Your ever loving son, Arthur.'

Well, that's a bit more like it. If the Huns intercept that one it'll give 'em something to think about.

*He stamps the letter and opens the one **Conor** has given to him. He peers at it for a moment, then groans.*

David Oh thanks Conor, that's really helpful. How am I supposed to censor a letter when it's all written in Gaelic?

*He stamps it anyway. **Bobby** enters.*

Bobby Have Peter and Clem got back yet?

David I don't think so. They're probably having a good time in some estaminet or other.

Bobby They'll be lucky if they find an estaminet that's still in one piece. Have you been into Wipers?

David Yes, I came through it on the way up. It's very sad, isn't it, the mess they've made of all those lovely old buildings. Still, c'est la guerre, as they say.

Bobby You've – um… you've got quite a talent for motivating the men. I've not seen them working this hard in months. I've left them all to it.

David I just try to behave like a human being, that's all. Works wonders.

Bobby What did you used to do for a living before the war?

David As little as possible.

Bobby   A gentleman of leisure, eh?

David   No, not exactly. Pater makes bicycles. I was supposed to follow him into the business but I turned out to be completely useless. Not a grain of business sense whatever. In fact I was so awful that I sacked myself. The only decent decision I ever made.

Bobby   You can't have been that bad, surely?

David   Well, it wasn't just that; the medico got a bit jittery as well. I've got TB, you see. My mother had it, she died just after I was born, and I turned out to be a bit of a crock myself. Spent half my childhood in splints, and I'm still a bit dodgy on the old pins from time to time, as you might have noticed. Then a couple of years ago it started up in my lungs again, and that was that.

Bobby   They let you into the army with TB?

David   Oh, they'll take anything that looks like it might be useable as an officer. I joined up at the beginning of 1915, when the expeditionary force had just had a right pasting and they were looking for people to train up as officers. I'm all right, really, not about to drop dead or anything; I just get a bit worried when they send the gas over. If I did get gassed it would probably finish me off, but in all honesty –

There is a brief whine and the crash of a shell exploding nearby. They both crouch down.

Bobby   That one was a bit close.

David   I hope Conor and Arthur are keeping their heads down out there.

Bobby   So do I. I worry about Conor a bit sometimes, he gets kind of nervous.

David   In what way?

Bobby   Well… I suppose he's just a very imaginative chap, really. He acts like he's got shellshock sometimes, but I don't think he has. No more than the rest of us anyway. He just gets very jumpy and starts seeing things. I don't think it's a problem particularly, but if he's had a shell drop on his head tonight out there don't be surprised if he comes back in a bit delirious.

David   If he's had a shell drop on his head I won't expect him to come back in at all.

Bobby   You know what I mean. Anyway, you were saying.

David   Was I? Oh yes. I joined up last year just to get out of the way at home, and – well, here I am.

Bobby You're Kitchener's Army, then?

David Absolutely. Thought I'd better sign up to do my bit before they started conscripting everybody.

Bobby We're all Kitchener's men too. What's left of us. Most of the lads who joined up the same time as us went down to the Somme. They nearly all got done in. The great British victory on the Somme, they're calling it in the papers, but when you see the casualty lists it makes you wonder, doesn't it?

David *(bitterly)* You don't have to tell me about the 'great British victory' on the Somme. I was in it.

Bobby Really?

David Mm. That's why they've sent me up here to a quiet part of the line, I suppose, to recover. I lost my whole platoon, Bobby. Every last man. Machine-gun fire.

A single rifle shot rings out a short distance away. They look at each other in alarm.

Bobby That sounded like one of ours.

David *(jumping up)* They must be in trouble...

Bobby *(jumping up and grabbing **David**'s arm)* Now don't go looking over the parapet again. You can't do anything. Just have to wait for them to come back in.

David Who's on sentry duty tonight?

Bobby Well, it's Conor's turn really, but Jerry's doing it for the moment. He won't have seen anything though, it's as black as Newgate's knocker out there. I shouldn't worry too much; if it was a British rifle then it probably just means they've bumped into a German patrol and let them have it. It happens from time to time. Not a very nice night to be out there, though. There's a lot of artillery stuff coming over. Are you still planning to go on patrol tonight?

David Oh yes. I'll be all right. I think it's all rather jolly, slithering about on one's stomach in the mud. It's the sort of thing that makes the men respect an officer.

Bobby True. But it doesn't do an officer much good to be respected if he's dead.

David Well thank you. I say, Bobby, if anything did happen to me out there... would you be able to send a message to my girl for me?

Bobby Sure. If you tell me what to say.

David   Yes, of course. Just say… *(he thinks for a moment)* just say 'Pip pip old fruit.'

Bobby   'Pip pip old fruit.' Is that all?

David   Yes. It's rather succinct, isn't it? Says everything that needs to be said. Would you do that for me?

Bobby   I should think so. Where does she live?

David   Coventry. You'll find her address stuffed down the back of the gramophone in my –

*He catches sight of **Conor**, who enters slowly from out of the darkness, alone. He trails his rifle along beside him and no longer carries the picket stakes and wire.*

David   Conor old man, are you all right?

Conor   I'm fine.

David   Where's Arthur?

Conor   Hit by a crump.

Bobby   Oh Jesus.

David   Is he dead?

Conor   *(with a touch of hysteria)* I couldn't do anything for him, there was nothing I could do.

David   It's all right, it's all right. Just tell me what happened.

Conor   I don't rightly know, it was all so quick. We were fixing up the wire and – and this thing just hit us. I 'clare to God it threw me six feet through the air. Arthur was a few yards further on and he copped it right enough. It wasn't a very big one but it came down right by him. He didn't stand a chance. We were unlucky, that's all. It was the only crump that came over this way and it bloody well got us.

David   We heard it come over. Now, you're quite certain he's dead?

Conor   *(grimly)* Oh ay, there's not much doubt about that.

David   All right. Did you stumble across any Germans out there? We heard a rifle shot just now.

Conor   No, I think that must have been a sniper taking a pot-shot at me, but I couldn't see anyone.

Bobby   Yes, they just let bang at random if they think there's a British patrol out there. They hardly ever plug anyone but they'll have a go anyway.

*David unfastens a small water-bottle from his belt and hands it to **Conor**.*

David   Go and sit in the big dug-out and have some of this.

Conor   What is it?

David   Whisky. Single malt.

Conor   Thanks. I'll take a little drop but I have to go up on sentry duty tonight.

David   You don't have to, Conor, you'd be better off having a rest for a while. One of the others will cover for you.

Conor   No, I want to. It'll help to take me mind off it. I want to be doing something useful.

David   All right. But you're to rest for an hour first. And that's an order, just for once.

*Conor goes out, and **David** motions for **Bobby** to go after him and keep watch on him. When he is alone he picks up **Arthur's** letter from the pile of censored mail, looks at it sadly and sighs. Then he rummages in his pocket and takes out a pen and pad of paper. Sitting down on the ammunition crate he pauses to think for a moment then begins to write.*

David   Dear Mrs Burrows…

*There is a strange semi-musical sound from off and **Peter** and **Clem** wobble onto the scene, very drunk. **Peter** has a small, cheap mouth-organ which he is attempting to play, very ineptly. **Clem** is clutching an empty wine bottle. They have had a good time and are in high spirits. **Peter** stops when he sees **David**, and **Clem** bumps into him, and they both grab each other to stop themselves from falling over.*

Peter   Watch out, you clumsy bugger.

David   *(writing)* It is my very sad duty…

Clem   You nearly had me over then.

David   … to inform you…

Peter   I didn't touch you, you silly sod, you just weren't looking where you were going.

David   … that your son Arthur…

Clem   You nearly made me spill my van.

David   …was killed this evening…

Peter   There isn't any van in there, you've drunk it all. *(he snatches the bottle from **Clem** and tips it up to show that it is empty)*

David   … while mending the wire in front of our trenches.

Clem	Here, give me that! *(he snatches the bottle back)*
David	It may be some comfort to you to know…
Peter	What you going to do, play a tune on it?
David	… that one of his friends was beside him when he died.
Clem	Hey, Peter. That woman with the raspberry bushes… *(**Peter** and **Clem** both burst out laughing)*
David	The only other consolation I can offer…
Peter	*(in a falsetto with a foreign accent)* Ze bloody Tommies, zey dessicate my raspberries! *(they both laugh again)*
David	… is an assurance that he was killed instantly…
Clem	I said to her, I said, she ought to try growing coconuts. Then maybe the Tommies would be doing her a favour, eh? *(they hoot with laughter)*
David	… and did not suffer any pain.
Peter	Silly old bat.
David	I enclose a letter which he wrote to you…
Clem	Come on Peter, let's have another tune.
David	… shortly before his death.
Peter	What do you want me to play?
David	On behalf of myself and all Arthur's friends and comrades…
Clem	Tipperary!
David	… I offer you my deepest sympathy.
Peter	I dunno how to do that one.
David	Yours sincerely…
Clem	Well we'll do one of mine then.
David	Second-lieutenant David Cartwright.
Peter	One of yours?
Clem	Yeah, listen to this, listen to this.

He clears his throat and begins to sing, a little tunelessly and very loudly.
***Peter** joins in with some random notes on the mouth-organ, because he doesn't know the tune.*

> Van roogy is good if you're feeling downhearted
> It makes you feel worse, makes you wish you were dead
> If I had a bottle I'd drink the whole damn lottle
> And stagger about and collapse on the bed.

Van roogy goes down like a crump in a rainstorm

They charge you the earth and they water the brew

If I had a bottle I'd drink the whole damn lottle

And play Madame's gramophone all the night through.

*At this point **Peter** goes into an upbeat solo in a different tempo, trying to
liven up the song and making a precarious attempt at doing a little dance,
which nearly causes him to fall over. **Clem** listens to a couple of bars and
tries to accompany him by blowing across the top of the wine bottle to get
a tuneless flute effect. After a little while he gets fed up and gives **Peter** a
slap to silence him. **Peter** stops playing and slaps him back. They stand in
disorientated silence for a moment, then **Clem** continues his song in the
same slow drawl.*

Van roogy leaves fur on your tongue and your larynx

Your uvula, your epiglottis and lips

If I had a bottle I'd drink the whole damn lottle

And send twenty mortar-bombs over to Fritz.

*By way of a coda he lilts the last line of the tune again and rises to a
wailing crescendo at the end. **Peter** attempts to outdo him in volume by
blowing the mouth-organ as hard as he can, irrespective of what note he is
playing. **Clem** retaliates by blowing across the top of the bottle as hard as
he can. Eventually they both run out of breath.*

David   Very nice, lads.

Clem   D'you like it? I just made it up.

Peter   You can't have just made it up, you sang it last year at the
Christmas do.

Clem   Shut up.

David   I'm afraid, chaps, I've got some rather sad news for you.

*There is a brief wailing sound and a shell explodes close by. All three get
down on the floor.*

Clem   Jesus, I wish they wouldn't do that.

David   It sounds as though we're not going to get any peace tonight.

Peter   *(getting shakily to his feet)* Peace? *Peace?* There's never any
peace anywhere. That's the whole point of having a bloody war,
isn't it?

From off comes the sound of an anxious voice calling "Stretcher-bearers! Stretcher-bearers!" They all listen, and it has a noticeable sobering effect on Peter and Clem.

Clem   Christ. Sounds like some poor sod's been hit.

Peter   This is a rotten bloody war. I don't know why we don't all just go home. I don't reckon the Germans enjoy killing us any more than we enjoy killing them.

Clem   Too right. Can we go home please, David?

David   If it was up to me then yes, but unfortunately we've got to stand here defending this pile of foul and useless rubble until we've all been killed and there's nobody left. Those are our orders.

Clem   Sod it.

Conor enters, sees Peter and Clem, and hesitates.

David   Did you want me for something, Conor?

Conor   I did. I was wondering if I could just have a word with you a minute.

David   Yes of course. *(to Peter and Clem)* I tell you what, boys, why don't you toddle off and have a drink of water and a lie down?

Clem   There isn't any water. The ration cart hasn't been up yet. We've only got that wine and Worcester sauce that we got for you.

David   Well how about taking it to my dug-out then, there's a good chap.

Clem   *(with an exaggerated salute)* Yessir.

Peter   We know when we're not wanted, eh Clementine? *(singing tunelessly)* Oh m'darling, oh m'darling…

Peter and Clem go out, somewhat shakily. David pulls over a crate for Conor to sit on. The sound of gunfire and distant explosions has become gradually louder and more frequent.

David   Here, pull up an ammunition crate. Mind you don't get splinters in your backside.

Conor   *(sitting)* Thanks. I was going to ask – would it be possible to get a padre sent down here?

David   What, now?

Conor   Yes. As soon as possible.

David   Well now, that's a thing I couldn't say. I know there is one around here somewhere but at this time of night he'll probably be out attending to burials.

Conor	Actually, no, I wasn't really thinking of him. He's Church of England.
David	Ah.
Conor	I was wondering if you could find a Catholic padre.
David	I wish I could, old man, but it might be a bit difficult out here. I mean, in the front line…
Conor	You're not a Catholic yourself by any chance?
David	No. Does it matter?
Conor	I don't know.
David	Why do you need to see a priest so urgently, if you don't mind my asking? Can anybody else help?
Conor	Ah no, it's nothing really, I just haven't seen one for a long time, that's all.
David	Do you really need to find one tonight? Could it wait until the morning?
Conor	*(without conviction)* Yes. Yes, it can wait till the morning. It doesn't matter.

*They sit in silence for a moment, then **David** reaches down and picks up a couple of pieces of sack from the floor. He carefully arranges one of them round his neck, places a smaller one on his head, and makes the sign of the cross in the air in front of him with his hand.*

David	In nomine Patris et Filii et Spiritus Sancti.
Conor	*(horrified)* You can't do that!
David	Why not? I've got a school cert in Latin.
Conor	You're not a priest.
David	No, I'm a human being with a warm heart and a sympathetic ear. Now off you go.
Conor	I can't make confession to an – *(he stops)*
David	What? An Anglican? An officer? An ordinary chap?
Conor	You wouldn't understand.
David	Oh but I do understand, Conor. I do. You see, it doesn't matter very much what you believe in. That absolution has to come from inside. A priest can't really do anything except help you to make peace with your own conscience. There's no reason why I can't assist you in that.
Conor	But you're not a priest. You're not even a Catholic.

David   I believe in God. That's a start.

Conor   No it isn't.

David   Listen. Listen. *(he pauses and listens to the guns)* There's a war on out there, Conor. Different rules apply in war. If a dirty great five-nine comes down on our heads tonight we're all going to be up there presenting our case to St. Peter and I don't think he's going to throw you out just because there weren't any priests available.

Conor   You don't know that.

David   I don't think either of us is in a position to know anything, but that's no reason not to have a bit of faith. Look, I can't find you a padre, but I can see that you need help, there's something troubling you that you need to talk about. I'm a good listener and an impartial judge and that's the best you're going to get.

Conor realises that he doesn't have much choice. After a pause he reluctantly gets down on his knees, turning slightly so that he doesn't have to look at David.

Conor   Bless me f– *(he pauses to think of a suitable substitute for 'Father', but unable to find one he just carries on)* – for I have sinned.

David   Haven't we all. Come on, see if you can shock me.

Conor   It concerns Arthur.

David   I wondered if it might.

Conor   *(getting nervous)* Look, is this going to be in strict confidence? I mean, you are my platoon commander, and if you think this is really terrible –

David   It's all right, I'm temporarily suspending my officer status. I give you my word.

Conor   Well, it's about Arthur.

David   Yes. All right. Take your time.

Conor   His death. It wasn't an accident.

David   Wasn't an accident?

Conor   No. I shot him.

David   Holy God.

Conor   Do you think that's terrible?

David   Well, I –

Conor	I didn't want to do it. There was nothing else I could do for him.
David	Just a minute, just a minute. *Why* did you shoot him, exactly?
Conor	Because he asked me to.
David	*(taken aback)* I see. Might one enquire as to why he may have wanted to be shot?
Conor	He was bleeding. Really terrible. I couldn't do anything for him.
David	Hang on, hang on. I think it might be best if you were to tell me exactly what happened out there. From the beginning.
Conor	I told you the first bit already. We were mending the wire. I was putting the stakes in and he was following along behind with the wire. It's a slower job, doing the wire, so I got some way in front of him. Then this bloody crump come over. You know by the noise that it's coming right at you. You only hear it for a moment, but you know. I heard this thing coming so I tried to get down but there wasn't really any cover out there, and not any time either. The next thing I knew I was blasted right off me feet. At least I fell away from the wire, and by some miracle or other I didn't get wounded, though I really thought I was done for. There was all this hot shrapnel dropping all around me but nothing hit me. So I got out me torch and went back to see if Arthur was all right, and he was lying on the edge of this crater where the shell had come down. It can't have been a very big shell but it made a bloody awful mess of him. Both his legs were just – gone. Just like that. And he'd got shrapnel wounds in his chest and face. He was just lying there on his back at the side of this hole and the blood was pouring out of him, everywhere, horrible.
David	Yes, go on.
Conor	Well, he was conscious, but he was in such terrible pain, and he was trying really hard not to cry out in case the Boche heard it. He was dying. I saw it in his eyes. It was like some light had gone out. But I had me first field dressing and I started to get it out, you know, just to try to stop the blood. And he looked at me, and he said 'shoot me.' I said I couldn't do that, I'd have to go and get help, get him down to the aid-post. He shook his head and pleaded with me to shoot him. 'I'm finished,' he said, 'and I can't stand the pain.' And he was in pain too, he was in a terrible bad way. He was begging me. And all the time the blood was pouring out of him in these horrible rhythmic pulses. So I put me rifle up to his head and I shot him. And that was that. Do you think that's terrible?

David	No. No, I don't.
Conor	He was just bleeding to death. They wouldn't have been able to do anything for him, would they?
David	No. Not with wounds like that. It would only have prolonged his suffering, and they wouldn't have been able to save him.
Conor	He was in such pain. I'd never have been able to do it otherwise.
David	It's all right, Conor, you did the right thing.
Conor	Do you think so?
David	Yes I do. And I can absolve you of your sin in the name of any religion you like.
Conor	*(sobbing with relief)* God, I felt so awful about it. I wish I could have done something for him.
David	You did the only thing possible in the circumstances.
Conor	I wanted to bury him, but you can't really, not out there. I just had to leave him.
David	I know, I know. It doesn't matter, Conor. Not now.
Conor	Thank you. For making me talk about it.
David	That's all right. Would you like me to set you a few Hail Marys and Paternosters as a token gesture or will that be enough?
Conor	I think I'll be all right now, thanks.
David	Are you sure you're up to doing sentry duty tonight?
Conor	Oh ay, I'd like to get on with something normal. I don't think I'd get much sleep tonight anyhow.
David	Right-o. But I'm off out on patrol myself shortly, so don't shoot *me*, there's a good chap.
Conor	*(laughing)* I'll try not to. *(turning serious again)* How come you always make jokes about things like that?
David	Oh, it's a way of coping with things. A good sense of humour is important. The war puts things like that in perspective.
Conor	I suppose it does. You've got to have a laugh about death, haven't you? Otherwise you'd go mad.
David	Absolutely. It's so much easier if you're mad to start with. It's less of a shock then.
Conor	There's just one other thing I have to tell you.
David	What's that?
Conor	Priests don't wear hats.

David   *(whisking the bit of sack off his head)* Oh, I'm terribly sorry.

Conor   Don't worry about it. It suits you.

David   Does it? Right-o, I'd better wear it then. Rather more fetching than those rotten old tin hats, what? *(he puts it back on)* I'm going to have to push off if I'm going to have a sniff round the Boche trenches tonight. *(calling)* Sammy! *(to Conor)* I wish Fritz would leave off that infernal racket. A fellow can hardly hear himself think.

Conor   Ay, it gets like that sometimes. Drives you mad. You feel like just going over there and telling them to shut up.

David   Mm. What a splendid idea.

Sammy enters.

David   Sammy, old top. Can you find me a couple of big bits of wood and some chalk?

Sammy   The chalk's no problem. I'll see what I can do about the wood. *(he exits)*

David   Good-oh. *(to Conor)* If you'd like to take up the sentry position at this post here I'll go and tell Jerry he can knock off for the rest of the night. But if you get tired and need to have a break just give me a shout.

Conor   Thank you sir – David.

David   *Sir* David now, is it? Steady on, you'll give me ideas above my station.

*He goes out the same way as **Sammy**. **Conor** climbs up into position on the firestep. The guns are louder than ever. The fragile state of his nerves is obvious as he crouches behind the parapet. There is a pause.*

Conor   Please God, grant there'll be no more bombs tonight. Is there never going to be any peace anywhere in this godforsaken world? It's like the surface of the moon out there, pocked and battered and jagged. Our forests are splintered stumps, our ponds and rivers are craters sick with phosgene, our birds are bursting shrapnel, our flowers are the rosy stains on dead men's tunics. The sky is an arc of black flame, the stench of cordite and cancer. The only language men know now is the chatter of machine-guns, the bursting of crumps. Whizz-bang, whizz-bang, they all fall down. There's a death here that goes beyond the bodies that writhe and twitch in the mud. There's a death of the soul of man, the final fall of Adam.

David and Sammy enter. David is carrying a large wooden signpost with 'QUIET PLEASE' chalked on it. He still wears the sack on his head. Conor is startled by their entrance and nervously swings his rifle towards them.

Conor   Who's that? Who's there?

David   It's me, you silly ass. With Sammy. What did you think we were, Mons angels?

Conor   You caught me by surprise.

David   We're just on our way out. *(indicating the signpost)* I thought I'd pop this up in front of Fritz's trench. Might give him the message.

Conor   *(incredulously)* You're going to put *that* in front of the Boche trenches?

David   Yes, why not?

Conor   Do you think they'll understand it in English?

David   Oh, I think they'll get the gist all right. It'll give 'em something to look at in the morning besides half a mile of festering swamp. If we're not back in two hours you'd better raise the alarm. Otherwise we'll see you at breakfast tomorrow morning. Toodle-pip.

David and Sammy go out. Conor shifts to get comfortable on the firestep. The thundering of the guns continues.

Conor   God, it's a horrible night. Nothing but guns, guns, guns. It was a horrible night for you, Arthur, right enough. And what are you feeling now? Are you glad to be out of the war? No more crouching in trenches knee-deep in muddy water with the crumps raining shrapnel on you. No more working parties out in No Man's Land, stumbling over wire and slimy corpses. No more army biscuits, no more plum and apple jam. No more lice, no more swollen feet. No more standing with your heart in your mouth waiting for the whistle to blow, no more marching towards the guns. Is it quiet enough where you are now? Or do you still hear them booming out anger and death over half of Europe? The whole world's gone mad. None of us is going to get out of this alive, you're lucky to be out of it now. And David – he's a nice feller – can't they spare him? And Sammy, he's only a lad, they can't take him, can they? *(looking out into No Man's Land)* Are you there, Arthur? I think I can see you – can't you come a little closer? Arthur, I see the fire in the earth. I don't like it at all. They'd swallow a man up, those terrible gaps. Now mind where

you're going Arthur, do you not see the great red crack just there?
There! It's full of men already, heaps and heaps of men, all dead.
Why is the earth full of fire, Arthur? What's going to become
of the dead? Are they all damned by their actions for King and
Country? Or is it only their own consciences that damn them?
Arthur, why don't you answer? Why do you look at me like that?
*(he turns and looks up at the sky, and a warm light shines onto his
face)* Yes, yes, I can see it too. A sun in the Western sky. Did you
ever see the sun like that, Arthur? You could almost breathe it in. I
can see the lady too – robed in light and holding up the golden sun
to call all the dead soldiers home. Do you know what this means,
Arthur? It means it's over, the game is over. Whizz-bang, whizz-
bang, they all fall down. It's time for them to rise up now, the
game's over. *(commandingly)* Let the dead arise! Out of the shell
craters, out of the mud, out of the filthy slime, let the dead arise!
Out of the broken trees, out of the barbed wire entanglements,
out of the wrecked trenches, let the dead arise! Out of the burning
earth, let the dead arise! Let the undead arise! Rise up now, see
that light in the West. Kick the filth of battle from your heels and
rise up. Follow the western splendour. Go! Go to the real Western
Front!

Blackout.

ACT TWO, SCENE ONE

The scene opens with a scratchy gramophone recording of Roses of Picardy *(ideally this should start as soon as the houselights have gone down and before the stage-lights come up, so the audience are listening to it in total darkness for a short while). As the lights come up on the scene they reveal the same trench a few days later. Everything is much tidier and brighter. On the right-hand side is a good-sized dug-out with a sack hanging over its entrance stamped with the words 'Post Office Property. Not To Be Taken Away.' Above this is a sign with 'Pemberley' chalked on it in fancy lettering.* **Sammy** *sits just in front of it, engrossed in polishing a regimental badge. It soon becomes apparent that the music is coming from a gramophone inside the dug-out. A moment later the sack is brushed aside and* **David** *emerges, dancing with emotional vigour, and holding up his 'partner', which comprises a rifle draped with a trench-coat and with a tin hat balanced on the top. As the song draws towards a close* **Bobby** *enters, with* **Peter**, **Clem** *and* **Jerry** *in tow. He holds a leather-bound notebook.* **David** *stops dancing and casts his 'partner' aside.*

David   Aa-ah, I love that song.

Clem   We'd gathered that. You've played it eight times today already.

David   Nine.

Bobby   We were just going to ask you whether you could speak German.

David   Now there's a thing to ask a chap. Yes, as it happens, you're in luck. I know a good bit, anyway.

Jerry   There, you see? I told you he could.

Bobby holds out the notebook to **David**.

Bobby   We were just sorting through Arthur's things, and came across this. He showed it to us just before he was killed. It's a German diary which he salvaged from a dead Hun last time we had a trench raid. We had a look at it but none of us could read it. It's in German.

David   Well, it would be. Let's have a look.

He thumbs through the notebook and begins to translate one of the entries. **Sammy** *puts his polishing aside and comes over to listen.*

David   'Wednesday 21st June 1916. The English continually pound our line with their heavy field guns. When will it ever stop? Our officers are sheltering now in the deeper dug-outs, and we must hold the line with only the wooden shelters to protect us from the shells. We are safe from the falling shrapnel but if any shells fall in the trench we are finished, and we dare not venture out. For hours we crouch in these dingy holes with the ground shaking all around us. I begin to give up hope of ever seeing Lotte and Anneliese again. In this hell of bursting bombs it is impossible to get any message through to our loved ones. Jürgen Meyer was buried alive in his dug-out and it will be a week or more before his young wife hears of it. We heard his screams but could not leave our shelter to go and help him, it is certain death to go out under this barrage. I wish the war was over and we could all go home. The English do not want to kill us and we do not want to kill them. It is a war of madness.'

Peter   *(delighted)* Well! How about that! The Huns are getting demoralised!

Clem   We'll have the buggers on the run in no time now!

Peter   Chase the dirty bastards all the way back to Berlin!

Sammy   Stick a rifle-grenade up the Kaiser's arse!

Jerry   And set a match to the whole bloody lot!

David   Before you get too excited, chaps, I ought to point out that I've read quite a few letters from you lot that weren't too dissimilar to this.

Peter   Well… not like that exactly.

David   'I wish the war was over and we could all go home.' I recall you saying something like that yourself not so long ago.

Peter   *(defensively)* I was drunk. I didn't mean it.

Sammy   You write that sort of stuff in your poems too.

Peter   Shut your face.

David   I didn't know you were a poet, Peter.

Sammy   Yeah, he's really good. Go on, read us that one you were doing this morning.

Peter   I haven't finished it yet.

Sammy   It was good though.

Bobby   Yeah, come on Peter, we like hearing your poems.

David   It's either that or I'll go and wind up the trench gramophone again.

Peter   *(pleased to be asked but trying desperately not to show it)* Oh all right then. *(he takes a scrap of paper from his pocket and unfolds it)* It's a sort of a sonnet, but it went a bit wrong in the middle. It's called No Known Graves.

Clem   Oh, a nice cheerful one then.

Peter

Is this the only trophy of the fight?
A newspaper's laconic afterword
On thousands lost, expunged, unsepulchred
And massacred for what we think is right?
How can a page of listed names requite
A trampled muddy body uninterred,
A pain that ripped the mind, the senses blurred,
The scarlet splash, the quenching of the light?
So elegies in ink must be the token
Of their loss; they have no chance to say
The truth, the fear, the sufferings unspoken,
And time will thin the memories away.
They brought no dawn to chase the foggy grey;
Their tears are dry, their last defence is broken.

Sammy   You see? I told you he was good.

Clem   I don't understand it.

David   Survive this war, Peter. You've got to survive this war.

Peter   Well, I'll try.

David   I mean it. Whatever happens to the rest of us, make sure you get safely home and keep writing those poems. What we've seen and done out here must never be allowed to be forgotten. Never. From generation to generation, people have got to go on being reminded of it.

Clem   Speak for yourself, I *want* to forget it.

David   Yes but can't you see, Clem, that unless people remember this war then it will all just keep happening over and over again. As civilisation plods on, wars of this scale will just get easier and easier to set up, and harder to stop.

Sammy   No, I don't see it like that. Nobody's going to want another war again, not now, not after this. Nobody's that stupid as to want to go through this again. *(he sits down and resumes his polishing)*

Jerry   At this rate there won't be anyone left to fight another war anyway.

David   Ah well, who knows? I suppose we ought to concentrate on getting through this war before we start worrying about the next one.

Sammy   It's a funny thing about that diary though – it reminds me of something Conor was talking about the other day. He said he'd had a dream about this German bloke stuck in a dug-out with all the shells dropping on his head, writing about how much he missed his wife. Really vivid, it was.

Jerry   God, that's nothing. Remember that time we got into the Boche trench at Plugstreet? Conor and me was going along this trench – it was one of those with a traversing bit every twenty yards or so – and it was all clear. I was just about to run round the next bendy section, when all of a sudden Conor grabbed hold of my tunic, nearly pulled me over. Well, I called him a couple of names, 'cause you know what it's like when you're all tensed up in a situation like that, you can do without some prat suddenly grabbing you from behind. But he was deadly serious and signalled me to be quiet, and he had that funny look on his face, you know, like he does... sort of...

(He strikes a rather rigid, goggle-eyed pose)

Clem   Yeah, the constipated frog, you mean.

Jerry   Yeah. Well anyway, he gets this Mills bomb off his belt and pulls the pin out. And I'm thinking he's going to kill us both, he's finally dropped his marbles or something. But he stands there with this grenade, calm as you like, and then pops it over the wall of the traverse. And a minute later – or a couple of seconds later, rather – there's this big bang and a lot of dirt and stuff comes down, and we go round the other side of the traverse and there's this German officer lying there, dead, with his pistol still in his hand. He'd been stopped by Conor's bomb.

(There is a pause while the others wait for a punchline)

Sammy   *(expectantly)* Yeah?

Jerry   But don't you get it? Conor stopped me going round the corner because he knew that officer was there.

Peter   Well he can't have done, can he? It was a lucky guess, that's all.

Jerry Well it gave me the shits I can tell you. If he hadn't stopped and lobbed that bomb over the wall we would both have got our arses shot off.

Bobby Talking of which, have you heard how Major Ramsbotham is?

David opens his mouth to reply but is distracted by a chorus of sniggers from the men.

Bobby *(sternly)* It isn't funny.

This elicits a second, louder round of sniggers and snorts.

David He's in a rather bad way, I know that much. Blinded for sure and might lose an arm as well. They fished quite a bit of shrapnel out of him, by all accounts.

Peter How is he going to explain it to his friends back in Blighty? *(the four of them laugh again)*

David It was, I suppose, just a little unfortunate, but it could just as easily happen to any of us. A latrine-sap is a legitimate military target.

Clem What a way to go, though. Blown up on the crapper…

David *(feigning squeamishness)* Clem, please…

Bobby Get out of my sight you revolting men. Go and fetch the post. Go on, hop it.

Clem and Peter go out, amid much sniggering and scatological gestures. Sammy continues his work, trying not to laugh, until Bobby gives him a filthy stare which sends him scuttling into the dug-out.

Bobby Well? Have you decided what to do yet?

David About Conor, you mean? No, not really. I want to do what's best for him, but I'm not sure what that is.

Bobby He's still very jittery. I can't have him on sentry duty, it's hopeless. He's a bloody wreck.

David Hmm. Well, obviously officially I'm putting him down as a neurasthenia case. Shellshock.

Bobby What do you mean, 'officially'? What else could it be?

David Well I don't know, that's why I can't decide what to do with him.

Bobby His nerve's all gone, that's all. Could happen to any bloke who saw one of his mates get blown up by a shell. Especially a sensitive chap like him.

David   No, there's more to it than that. The thing is, Bobby, I can't decide whether he really is just a simple shellshock case or whether he's some kind of natural psychic.

Bobby   You're not serious?

David   Oh yes I am. There's a very fine dividing line between the two.

Bobby   You don't mean you think he really did see visions of the Virgin Mary floating about over a trench?

David   It was real enough to him.

Bobby   He's in shock. He can't even drink a cup of tea without slopping it all over himself, he's so nervy. And that's not a symptom of being psychic.

David   Maybe. I think perhaps I should try to send him home.

Bobby   He won't go. Not back to Ireland.

David   Why ever not?

Bobby   Has he told you about his brother?

David   No.

Bobby   You know there was some trouble over in Dublin around about Easter time? Some chap went into the post office to buy a stamp and got so bored waiting in the queue that he decided to shoot the place to pieces and declare himself the leader of a new Irish Republic?

David   Well, yes, I'm not sure it was quite like that, but I know they had a rebellion over there.

Bobby   Yes, well, Conor's brother – Liam, or whatever his name was – took part in the Rising, and was shot by a British soldier. Rumour has it that he was unarmed and tending a wounded comrade when it happened, and so he's become something of a local martyr. Naturally Conor's position out here is not very well regarded by his family. He's basically fighting for the people who killed his brother. Not a nice thing to have to live with.

David   Why on earth did Conor enlist in the British army if he comes from an Irish Nationalist background?

Bobby   I've never really thought to ask him.

David   No, I suppose one wouldn't. Well, I can see why he might not feel very comfortable about going back to Ireland. I wonder whether I can get him carted off to some hospital or other in England?

Bobby Anyway, I hope this might help to explain a bit about why he's in the state he is. I mean, he's spent a year out here with bombs and bullets flying round his ears the whole time, and he doesn't feel he can go home anymore because his family won't have him. It's all been grinding him down bit by bit, and the business with Arthur just broke him. It happens.

David Yes, yes, I see. Thank you for telling me. It does help to put it in perspective. *(he looks round to check that **Sammy** isn't within earshot)* Look, there's something I've got to tell you now, Bobby. It's confidential for the moment, all right?

Bobby Yes of course.

David We're making an attack. A daylight attack. This afternoon.

Bobby Oh God.

David I had the orders yesterday, under strict instruction not to tell the men until the last minute. I hate keeping things from them, but you know how they blab, I couldn't afford to chance it. So you see why I need to make a decision about Conor fairly quickly.

Bobby Yes. Yes, I see. What's the purpose of the attack?

David I don't know. Some general or other with nothing better to do than sit around making silly plans, I suppose. At any rate – and this really is confidential, by the way – we're only there to protect the flank of D Company. But on no account are the men allowed to know that. They have to be made to believe at all times that they are main protagonists in the fight. Those were my orders.

Bobby A daylight attack, though. Is that wise, from a position like this?

David Wise? It's not wise at all, it's suicide. But that's what they've told us to do. *(he takes a map from his pocket and shows it to **Bobby**)* This is where we are, here. Our first objective is to take this little blob over here, Caterpillar Farm. To get to that we have to slog through at least two lines of German trenches – here and here. Then we have to advance through Squelch Valley, bearing north a bit...

Bobby Squelch Valley? That sounds –

David Wet. Yes. And our second objective is to enter Cold-iron Copse from the bottom left-hand corner, which presumably by then will be occupied by the survivors of D Company. At least that's the theory.

Bobby   Are we getting any back-up? I mean tanks or aircraft or what-not?

David   I think it's a bit more informal than that, old boy. They're going to have a five-minute artillery barrage in the run-up to zero hour, which supposedly will clear those two trenches of hostile Huns, and then we're on our own. It's a bullets and bayonet job, I'm afraid. And before you say anything, yes I do know it's ridiculous to attempt such a manoeuvre without a Lewis gun team. Don't think I haven't been bashing my head against the brick wall of army administration complaining that we need Lewis guns. We're on the waiting list, apparently.

Bobby   And the government is trying to make out that there isn't a munitions shortage…

David   Well, there isn't really. Just a slight hiccup in the distribution. We've got enough Mills bombs to blow up half of Belgium.

Bobby   It's better than nothing.

David   According to our dear friends at HQ the plan is to consolidate the Cold-iron Copse position by nightfall. That means we'll have to dig in as soon as we get there and get some semblance of a trench round the edge of the wood as quickly as possible.

Bobby   Excuse me for being a pessimist, but won't the Germans come straight back as soon as it gets light and massacre the lot of us, trench or no trench?

David   Well spotted, Bobby, you've found the unfortunate hitch in our strategy. It is indeed, in my opinion, a physical impossibility to consolidate a wood of that size by nightfall. Woods are bad news at the best of times. Though I understand Cold-iron Copse isn't really much of a wood these days, more a collection of frazzled stumps positioned in moderately close formation. Still, mustn't be downhearted. It's also my opinion – unofficially, of course – that we won't be going to Cold-iron Copse at all, so I shouldn't fret too much about whether we can or can't consolidate it.

Bobby   What do you mean?

David   Well frankly, with a fatuous battle strategy like this, D Company will be in retreat more or less before we have a chance to get out of our trenches, and barring any casualties we'll all finish up the day exactly where we started. Here in this trench.

Bobby   Great.

David So don't bother to pack your bags. We'll be home in time for tea.

Peter and Clem enter excitedly, carrying a fairly large parcel.

Peter Hey, look what we've got!

Clem A big food parcel courtesy of Arthur's mum!

Bobby You can't have that!

Clem Why not?

Bobby It isn't yours, it isn't addressed to you.

Peter Well it's not much good to Arthur now, is it?

Bobby That's not the point. You should show a little more respect for the dead.

Peter But a food parcel is only of any use to the living. What's the point of wasting it when we're all out here trying to live on stale bread and army biscuits?

Bobby If the person it's addressed to is deceased then it should rightfully be returned to the sender.

Clem Come on, Sarge. Arthur would want us to have it.

David Yes, Clem's right. If it's a food parcel there's no point sending it back to England. Far better to make use of it by distributing it between Arthur's friends. But any personal correspondence you find inside it must be returned unopened, along with any personal gifts.

Clem Yessir!

Peter and Clem begin to scuttle off with the parcel, but halt as David calls after them.

David Before you get too excited, I need you all back here right away, and that includes Jerry and Conor. Go and dump that in your dug-out if you want to, but come straight back.

Clem Yessir. *(they exit)*

David Incorrigible little fellows, aren't they? Very enterprising. Now where were we? Ah yes, the so-called advance on Caterpillar Farm. I suggest the men carry their rifles at the ready and take minimum pack, because survival is going to be of the old essence rather than all this messing about trying to dig holes. I would suggest an entrenching tool and a handful of Mills bombs should cover us for most eventualities. *(calling)* I say, Sammy!

Sammy emerges from the dug-out.

Sammy   Yes?

David   Did you stick the fuses in those Mills bombs, the ones in the big box?

Sammy   Just finishing them off now. *(he grins and holds out a partially dismantled hand-grenade)*

David   Jolly good. *(in a lower voice, to Bobby)* I can't see us getting far enough to be able to lob them at any Germans, but it'll make us all feel better to have our pockets stuffed with them.

Peter, Clem, Jerry and Conor enter, and stand ready. Sammy comes out of the dug-out and joins them. Conor looks pale and ill and a little dishevelled. His nerves are clearly not in good order.

David   Conor old man, how are you feeling?

Conor   I'm feeling fine thank you, David.

David   Good-oh. Now listen up, chaps, I've got something to tell you. Something important. We're making an advance this afternoon. It's nothing very spectacular, just a short artillery barrage and then we scurry swiftly across No Man's Land, lob a few hand-grenades at the Boche, and biff on to Caterpillar Farm, which, as I think you all know, is that pile of pulverised rubble just to the right of the German latrine-sap.

Peter   *(sarcastically)* Is that all?

David   From there we may or may not get further instructions to press on to a piece of woodland further up the valley, but I shouldn't worry about that for the moment. If you see any chaps charging around in khaki tunics don't shoot them, they're British. Probably members of D Company, who will be going over the top alongside us. If you see any chaps charging around in grey tunics don't let them shoot you. I shall be leading the attack, so make sure you follow me at all times. If I should cop it, Bobby will assume command and you must follow him. If Bobby cops it, throw yourself into the nearest shell-hole and wait for some friendly stretcher-bearers to come and retrieve you. If in doubt, pretend to be dead. In your case, Jerry, that shouldn't be difficult. Whatever you do, don't just stand around in front of the Boche machine-guns. Has everybody got that?

There is a murmur of nervous assent.

David   Right. Zero hour is at two thirty-two. Until then, just to keep your little minds occupied, we'll have a bit of drill on battle procedures. Come on, let's get this highly trained killing machine in motion. Fall in.

*The men get into line. **David** twirls his walking-cane and looks important. He gives his commands in an authoritative parade-ground bark, but clearly and audibly.*

David   Slope arms!

The men carry out the conventional parade-ground response of poising their rifles against their shoulders.

David   Prepare to advance!

The men pull stupid faces, bite their nails and knock their knees together in a show of mock nervousness.

David   Forward, and up!

The men mime the vigorous climbing of a ladder.

David   Evade fire!

The men duck and flinch to evade imaginary bullets just above their heads.

David   Forward, march!

The men run on the spot with exaggerated vigour.

David   Plug Hun!

The men raise their rifles with eager expressions and mime an attempt at firing, but there is no recoil.

David   Examine arms!

The men frown, put the stocks of their rifles against their ears and slap the barrel a few times, peer down the end, blow down it, turn the rifles upside-down and shake them as if to clear a blockage.

David   Have another go, plug Hun!

The men raise their rifles eagerly again and mime the firing and recoil. Then they grin, lick a finger and dab a line in the air with it as if chalking up a point.

David   Evade whizz-bang!

*The men look up with a hand cupped behind an ear and turn their heads slowly as if tracking something across the sky. **David** whistles in imitation of a falling shell, then stops abruptly.*

Bobby   Duck!

The men rapidly drop to the ground and crouch in a ball with their hands over their ears.

David   Up, and forward march!

The men get up and run on the spot, looking rather nervous.

David   Spot Maxim machine-gun. Panic.

The men open eyes and mouths in horror at the sight of an imaginary machine-gun, and flap their hands in terror.

David   Retreat, backward, quick march!

The men turn their backs and run on the spot with ridiculously exaggerated vigour, then take a jump forward, dropping to the ground as if landing from a great height, stand up, wipe the sweat from their brows, and all say in unison: "Phew, that was lucky!"

David   Excellent, excellent, I can see you've got all that down to a fine art. You'll have no problems at all out there on the battlefield this afternoon. All right, stand easy. Now, to get us all in the mood, we've just about got time for the platoon song.

They all launch into an unofficial version of 'Tipperary'. This is a polished performance and clearly the result of much practice. One of them pretends to be a trumpet, doing the intro and backing tune, while the others sing the song itself. At the end the chorus is repeated in two-part harmony.

> Submarines beneath the sea and zeppelins in the air
>
> Tons of Huns with great big guns, his soldiers everywhere;
>
> Said Bill 'I'll first take Calais, then for Dover O Mein Gott!'
>
> But Britain let her bulldog loose and fucked the bleeding lot
>
>
> It's a long way to get to Calais, it's a long way to go
>
> It's so damned far to get to Dover that you'll never stand the blow
>
> Goodbye German Empire, farewell Kaiser Bill
>
> If you don't know the way to hell God help you, you bleeding soon will.

David   Right-o then chaps, better get down to business. Go and get your rifles and kits sorted out.

*The men all go off, but **David** makes a gesture to **Conor** for him to remain behind.*

David   Conor, I'd like to have a quick word with you. That order doesn't include you. I'm withdrawing you from the attack.

Conor   What?

David   I'm putting you down as suffering from neurasthenia. You will go down to company headquarters with a note signed by me, and they will see to it that you get sent away to an English hospital for a while. Give you a chance to recuperate a bit.

Conor   *(half indignant, half joking)* You're not sending me to the loony bin, I'm not half so dotty as I look.

David   I know very well you're not dotty, Conor. I know what you saw, that night on the sentry post. But this war is breaking down your health and you need to get out of it for a while.

Conor   You don't know what you're doing.

David   It's my responsibility to look after the men in my platoon and I intend to do so.

Conor   David, you don't understand. I've served my purpose now.

David   Absolute rot. You're as valuable a soldier as anyone on the western front. And you're ill. You may not be barmy but you are ill.

Conor   Believe me when I say that I have to go out there and fight today. It's important.

David   Why? Does this have something to do with your brother?

Conor   Partly.

David   And what else?

Conor   This is the way it's got to happen. It's meant to be like this. Where my heart goes out I have to follow it. That's all.

David   Conor, I am your commanding officer. If I order you to withdraw from the attack and go down to the base then you will have no option but to obey me.

Conor   *(with cool confidence)* But you're not going to. Are you?

David   *(after a pause)* No.

Conor   Right. I'd better go and sort out my pack then.

David smiles sadly and pats him on the back as he goes out. **Sammy** *enters at the same time and gives* **Conor** *a bemused glance as he passes.*

Sammy   What's the matter with him? *(with a roguish grin)* Here, you'll never guess what.

David   No, I don't suppose I will.

Sammy   You're a very lucky chap.

David   Oh. Jolly good.

Sammy   When I was putting all our stuff together I thought to myself, I'd better just check David's service revolver, just make sure it's all in good order. And what do you think I found?

David   I dread to think. The rats haven't been at it again, have they?

Sammy   No, it's worse than that. *(he pauses for maximum dramatic effect)* It wasn't loaded.

David   Ah.

Sammy   *(he takes the revolver out of his pocket and brandishes it smugly)* If I hadn't thought to check it, you would have gone out into battle this afternoon unarmed.

David   Goodness.

Sammy   That would have given you a shock, wouldn't it, if you'd tried to plug a Hun and nothing came out?

David   Quite. How remiss of me.

Sammy   Well you needn't worry. I've put a full complement of bullets in it now. *(he hands the gun to* **David***)*

David   You're a good boy, Sam. Thank you.

Sammy   *(with mock ire)* What would you do without me, eh?

David   The mind boggles. *(he places the revolver in the holster on his Sam Browne)*

Sammy   I'll go and get the rest of the stuff. We're all ready now.

Sammy exits. **David** *stands and watches him with a smile. As soon as he is safely out of sight he takes the loaded revolver out of its holster again, opens it up and carefully shakes the bullets out into the palm of his hand. He looks furtively in either direction then hastily tosses the bullets over the parapet, and replaces the empty revolver in its holster.*

Bobby   *(from off)* Right, fix bayonets!

Clem   (*from off, singing*) We're here because we're here because we're here because we're here…

Peter   (*from off*) Shut your gob.

The men file in with ladders, which they place against the side of the trench. They straighten up their kit and clothing and stand in line, looking nervous but moderately cheerful.

David   Nervous?

Sammy   A bit, I suppose. But looking forward to strafing the Fritzes.

Bobby   (*looking at his watch*) Any minute now. Check safeties!

David   All right, chaps. Best of British and all that. And if the worst comes to the worst, just remember: Greater love hath no man than this, that a man get his chops blown off in a French trench.

There is a violent boom from off. They are momentarily startled, but it is only the start of the British artillery barrage. The guns build up to a crescendo.

David   Whoa, sounds like our artillery boys are doing the biz.

The sky begins to darken.

Peter   God almighty, we won't be able to see where we're going through all that smoke.

Jerry   That's probably just as well.

Bobby   Stand to, stand to.

The sky grows ever darker, and they increasingly have to shout over the noise of the guns.

Conor   (*fingering the crucifix on his rosary*) Holy Mother of God, pray for us.

David   Is there an aspect of God which presides over battles? Is there something we can pray to from this darkest chasm of human stupidity? Is there any divine love that can reach us here? Is there a light which can break through and cleanse the soul of man of this impulse to war which has caused so much needless suffering since the dawn of time?

Conor   Virgin most powerful, pray for us.

David   I ask no mercy for myself, only for the mothers who have given up their children. For the women who have given up the men they love and all their future happiness. For the civilians whose lives have been crushed and destroyed. For the doctors and nurses who have risked their own lives to redress some of the damage. For those who have watched their friends and colleagues die and been powerless to intervene. For the soul of the war-torn land.

Conor   Mirror of justice, pray for us.

David   I call on a higher mercy for the victims of conscience. For the ordinary soldiers whose sense of duty has forced them to kill one another against the inclinations of their nature. For the fighting men who believe their loyalty to King and Country has stained their souls irredeemably.

Conor   Star of the sea, pray for us.

David   Above all I ask mercy for the shellshock cases, the men for whom the horrors of war were so unbearably poignant that their minds and characters have been distorted out of recognition.

Conor   Mystical rose, pray for us.

David   Let our sacrifice this day be in perpetual memory of tainted conscience, of the staining of the land, and in everlasting remembrance of those lost in the ground.

Conor   Queen of peace, pray for us.

David   I commit myself to the service of the one and only light. Amen. Amen. Amen.

*The artillery barrage ceases abruptly. There is a moment of ringing silence, and then two or three whistles blow on either side, from off. **David** immediately blows his own whistle, and with some commotion they all scramble up the ladders, **David** first, armed only with a walking-cane, followed by **Sammy** and then the others. As they go over the top of the parapet they are met with a hail of machine-gun fire.*

Blackout.

ACT TWO, SCENE TWO

*The same scene, early in the morning. The noise of war has died down to a low, distant rumble. It is only just light, and **David** is writing – or trying to – with the aid of a small oil-lamp. He sits on the floor with the paper on top of an ammunition crate and the pen poised above it, but he leans his head on his hand and stares silently and motionlessly into the middle distance. **Clem** is poised similarly motionless on the embankment, on sentry duty. On the floor, **Peter** and **Sammy** lie wrapped in somewhat inadequate blankets. **Peter** has a bandage around his arm. There is a mess tin, a mug and a pan of water on an unlit tommy cooker on the floor nearby.*

Clem   *(in a tone of extreme boredom)* Oh joyous life… *(he yawns)* Is it waking up time yet?

Peter   Never.

Clem   I'm bored. Why doesn't Sam take a turn up here? Why is it always me?

David   *(without moving or looking up)* Because Sam is my servant. Servants don't do sentry duty.

Clem   Damned favouritism. I thought servants were supposed to polish buttons and bring their officers breakfast in the dug-out, not just lie around all morning.

David   Now then, there's no need to slander another man's servant. We want Flanders, not slanders.

Peter   We like having you on sentry duty, Clem, you're always so cheerful.

Clem   Why don't *you* come up here and do your bit, for that matter?

Peter   I can't do that, I'm the walking wounded.

Clem   No you're not, you're the prostrate-on-your-backside-wrapped-up-in-a-blanket-and-expecting-everyone-to-feel-sorry-for-you wounded.

Peter   Clem, I've been hit by a machine-gun.

Clem   Aah, shall we go and ask mummy to come and kiss it better?

Peter   You'll be kissing the end of my fist if you don't shut up.

Sammy gives a sad groan.

Peter   What's the matter with you?

Sammy	Nothing. I just can't believe that Conor's gone west, that's all.
Peter	Well he has, my boy. That's what happens when you have these here wars. People snuff it. Hey Clem, have you got any fags?
Clem	Not likely. I've got some tea, if you want to smoke that.
Sammy	No but I mean he was here yesterday, messing about and singing songs with us and everything. I can't believe I'm never going to see him again.
Clem	He's gone, Sammy. You don't get second chances with machine-guns. Peter got it in the same burst.
Peter	Yeah, I saw him go down, Sam. It was very quick.
Sammy	It's still not very nice. *(he sighs and begins to get up)*
Peter	Can you actually smoke tea? Have you tried it?
Clem	Oh yeah, loads of times. It's not very easy to roll, but it tastes all right.
Sammy	You're up early this morning, David.
David	I'm writing letters of condolence.
Peter	Well, you've only got two to do, that shouldn't take too long.
Sammy	*(horrified)* Peter!
David	It's the content, Peter, not the quantity.
Peter	You'd think the army would have a standard letter by now. 'Dear sir/madam, it is my most solemn duty to inform you that your brave and gallant son has been jerked to Jesus. Sorry and all that. Love from Georgius Rex.' Officers could be issued with a rubber stamp for King George's signature.
Clem	I would have thought it'll be something of a relief to Conor's parents. They wouldn't have wanted the embarrassment of having him come home in one piece at the end of the war.
David	Don't you believe it. A son is still a son.
Sammy	Jerry had a son, didn't he?
David	*(with a sigh)* Yes, thank you, Sam, for reminding me about that.
Peter	Now, if you think Conor hopped the twig quickly and painlessly, you should have seen Jerry go. That was style.
Sammy	You didn't see that as well, did you?

Peter   No, but my mate Redmond in D Company did. One of those dirty great black beggars, it was. Exploded right over him. Napoo Jerry Turner, just like that. Now that's got to be a good way to go. I bet he never even knew what hit him.

David   Unfortunately it doesn't make my task any easier.

Sammy   Well, he can't have felt any pain, can he? I'm sure his wife would like to know that.

David   Sammy, how do you tell a woman that her husband's body has literally been blasted out of existence?

They all sink into thoughtful silence.

Clem   It's such a shame about Conor. Nice feller.

David   He knew he was going to die. I was talking to him just before we went over the top. He didn't tell me in so many words, but he knew all right.

Peter   How can he have known? Nobody knows. It's just one of those things.

David   Maybe.

Peter opens the mess tin that is lying nearby and begins to roll a cigarette.

Sammy   You really think Conor had some kind of sixth sense, don't you?

David   Well, I don't know what it was exactly. It was that strange vision he had the night Arthur was killed. It sparked something for me. He told me he saw an image of the Blessed Virgin robed in gold, holding out the Christ child above her head, and that she seemed to be calling all the dead soldiers home. Now, when I first came out to the Front I was billeted in a French town called Albert, and the church there had a statue on the top that exactly matched Conor's description. A golden Virgin holding out the Christ child at arm's length. Very attractive it was, stuck up on the spire of a rather tastefully designed basilica. Anyway, at the beginning of last year Uncle Boche decided he didn't want us to be there any more and started hammering the place with shells. The golden madonna got knocked over at a ridiculous angle, somewhat below the horizontal, but stayed up there, leaning over the town as if she were on a clock-spring. It was quite spooky having to march along underneath her, because by then most of Albert was a bit of a mess and she looked as though she was about to cast the Christ child down into the rubble. Or was offering him in a gesture of blessing to the town, whichever way you look at it. Needless to say a plethora of ludicrous superstitions sprang up regarding what would happen if the golden madonna fell down, and it got so out of hand that the general staff sent a party of Royal Engineers up there to shore her up. For me that statue always symbolised the futility of war but also the light of hope that something could be salvaged and redeemed from it all. It just struck me as a little strange that Conor should have picked up on that identical image, having never been to Albert. That's all.

Sammy   He could have read about it somewhere.

David   He could have done. We'll never know now anyway.

Peter has lit his cigarette by now, takes a hefty drag, winces, and looks at it indignantly.

Peter   This is disgusting.

Clem   Try it with a bit of milk and sugar.

Peter   I think I will.

He tosses the cigarette contemptuously into a tin mug, pours some warm water on it from the nearby pan, and swirls it around.

Sammy   I'll miss Conor.

Peter   Yes. And it's not as if we even achieved anything in that stupid advance. More like a suicide excursion.

Clem   I think Peter had a very lucky escape though. Let's be grateful for small mercies.

Sammy   David had a lucky escape too. I saw him going straight towards one of the guns just waving his walking-stick at it. I think the Germans were so surprised they forgot to shoot.

David   Oh, I'm famous for my lucky escapes. When I was in the big push down on the Somme I got shot by a sniper at close range. Big nasty rifle bullet. Fortunately for me I had my cigarette case in my pocket and that's what the bullet hit – so hard that it stuck there and I couldn't get it out. The case was all bent and torn out of shape but it stopped the bullet so effectively that I wasn't even scratched. They've got a display of war artefacts in the town hall in my home town, and they asked me to donate the case, still with the Mauser bullet embedded in it. It's the pride of the collection. It's got a placard by it saying 'this cigarette case saved the life of a young British officer by protecting his heart from an enemy bullet'.

Sammy   Cor, that's really amazing.

David   Yes. Unfortunately they made a bit of an assumption about the location of the cigarette case on my person, and I've never had the courage to correct them. *(he grins and pats his bottom)* It was actually in my back pocket.

The men hoot with laughter. There is a cry of 'Sheepsrear!' from the other side of the parapet.

Clem   *(raising his rifle suddenly)* Christ, what was that? Oh, thank God, it's only Sarge coming in.

David   Oh good, I was beginning to wonder where he'd got to. Don't shoot him, Clem, for goodness sake, I can't afford to lose another non-commissioned officer.

Clem   Jesus, what is he playing at?

Bobby suddenly appears over the top of the parapet, slightly out of breath and quite unconcerned about his vulnerable position. He makes a playful grab at Clem's rifle.

Bobby   You're not going to believe this.

David   What?

Bobby   It's clear. The Germans have cleared out of those trenches. Both lines. It's deserted.

David   Surely not.

Bobby   It's true. I've been crawling around out there all night in front of the Boche trenches and there was no noise at all, nothing. So I went in and had a look around, and it's all just been abandoned. There were a few dead Germans knocking about but that's all. I found half eaten plates of food, a letter left off in mid-sentence, even a pile of half finished jam-tin bombs which somebody had been filling with shrapnel. Everything's been left exactly as it must have been at zero hour yesterday afternoon when they suddenly realised they were under attack. And that's not all. Several of the dug-outs had been deliberately blown up. It wasn't just lucky strikes from British shells, they'd been systematically bombed to block up the entrances. So they're obviously not intending to come back to them. They've destroyed them so that we can't make use of them.

David   Are you absolutely certain there aren't any 'pockets of resistance', as the official memos call them?

Bobby   Positive. Otherwise I wouldn't have been so daft as to come over the parapet in daylight, would I?

Sammy   But the attack failed. Why would they retreat when they know damned well they had us on the run?

David   There might be any number of tactical reasons for making a withdrawal which we couldn't possibly guess at. They might be concentrating their resources on building a stronger defence somewhere else. It could be that they misjudged the strength of our resources.

Peter   It could be a trap.

David   Indeed. We don't have any way of knowing except to get some men over there as quickly as possible. I'll go straight down to company HQ now and get further instructions. I'm sure you lot can find something to amuse yourselves for five minutes.

*David exits hastily. **Sammy** wanders over and has a surreptitious peep at the letter **David** had been writing. While he is standing there looking at it, **Clem** carefully hoists **Peter** up in a piggy-back and runs straight at him.*

Peter   Look out, Sammy, there's a tank coming!

*They barge into **Sammy**, almost knocking him over.*

Peter   Mind my frigging arm!

Sammy   Two against one? That isn't very fair.

Peter   Well you can be the cavalry or something.

Sammy   Cavalry against tanks? That isn't very fair either.

Clem   C'est la guerre.

*Clem circles round and begins to run at **Sammy** again, making roaring noises. **Peter**, still on **Clem**'s back, pretends to be operating a machine-gun. Just before they get to him, **Sammy** darts away at a canter as if he is on a horse. They continue to frolic like young children, **Sammy** snorting and frisking as he canters around the stage, **Clem** and **Peter** chasing after him making tank and machine-gun noises. After a while **Sammy** finds himself cornered and is forced to reverse – a manoeuvre which causes him to ram accidentally into **Bobby**, who is sitting on the firestep behind him.*

Bobby   Oi, watch where you're bloody going.

Peter   C'est la guerre.

Bobby   *(his scowl turning into a grin)* Come on Sammy, let's get 'em!

Bobby leaps to his feet and begins to canter childishly in the same manner as Sammy. They dart around the 'tank' and 'shoot' sporadically at it with imaginary revolvers, rather more like cowboys than cavalry. The 'tank' being somewhat more cumbersome (and in consideration to Peter's bad arm) wheels around more slowly, attempting to barge into the 'horses' to knock them over and machine-gunning them all the while. Finding himself cornered, Bobby scrambles up the embankment, canters friskily and fearlessly along the parapet, neighs roguishly and jumps back down at the other end.

Peter   *(sarcastically)* Oh, very clever.

Bobby   Come on, you old heap of junk.

The 'tank' makes a concerted charge at Bobby, who suddenly runs straight at it making alternate motorbike and machine-gun noises. They narrowly avoid collision, which almost unbalances the 'tank'.

Bobby   Sorry, the cavalry have had to stop using horses now. They've all defected to the Motor Machine Gun Corps.

Peter   Hey, that's not fair.

Bobby   C'est la guerre.

Bobby charges at them again, and a fierce battle ensues between tank and motorcycle. Sammy, still cantering around on his 'horse', begins to feel a little left out. Suddenly he jumps up on the embankment, spreads his arms out sideways, and roars along pretending to be an aeroplane.

Sammy   You're done for now. The Royal Flying Corps has arrived.

He charges along the parapet, dipping and swerving at the 'tank' to drop 'bombs' on it. The 'tank' wheels around in confusion. Suddenly Bobby hurls himself melodramatically on the floor.

Bobby   Wah! He's got me!

He 'dies' slowly and noisily. The others continue the battle. Sammy turns round and hurtles enthusiastically back along the top of the trench, bearing down on the helpless 'tank'. A rifle shot rings out from somewhere, and Sammy drops down on the far side of the embankment. It takes a moment for the others to realise what has happened.

Clem   What was that?

Bobby   He's messing about.

Clem   I thought I heard a rifle shot.

Peter   So did I.

Bobby   He's just trying to frighten us, that's all.

Clem   I'm not so sure. *(calling)* Sammy!

Bobby   Come on, Sam, don't bugger about.

Peter   *(to **Bobby**)* Why don't you go up there and have a look?

Bobby realises with gradually spreading horror that he is afraid to go up on the parapet.

Bobby   Shit. He really has gone, hasn't he?

Clem   What do we do?

Peter   Go and get David.

Bobby   Forget it. There's nothing David can do.

Clem   We can't just leave him.

Bobby   Well, there's a bloody medal in it for anyone who fancies going out there and bringing him in.

Clem   We can't just leave him. *(he jumps up onto the firestep, but the others grab him and hold him back)*

Peter   Don't be silly, Clem, you'll get shot.

David enters, and sees immediately that something is wrong.

David   What's happened?

Bobby   We think Sammy's been shot by a sniper. He's down the other side of the parapet.

David   What was he doing on top of the parapet? Oh never mind.

David jumps onto the firestep and takes a look over the parapet. A shot rings out and he ducks down.

Peter   David, for Christ's sake!

David   I can see him. He's down by the edge of the wire. If I could just slip over the top...

Bobby   *(grabbing **David**'s arm)* Don't do it, David. There's no point in two of you getting killed. We can go out and find him at nightfall.

David   He's only a child, Bobby. I'm not leaving him.

David pulls a large white handkerchief out of his pocket and waves it tentatively but urgently over the top of the parapet. Nothing happens, so he cautiously makes his way up onto the top of the trench, still waving the handkerchief. He has just raised his head and shoulders above the parapet when a shot rings out. He drops back down onto the firestep.

Bobby *(rushing over to him)* Oh my God –

David It's all right, Bobby. He missed.

He slowly climbs back up and waves the handkerchief over the top again.

David *(more to himself than anyone else)* Now don't shoot me, there's a good chap.

Very slowly and carefully he raises himself onto the parapet, waving the handkerchief continuously. The others wait in agonised suspense.

David Don't shoot, don't shoot. Good man.

By now he is on top of the trench, completely exposed to the sniper. He pauses for a few agonising moments but there are no further shots. He stuffs the white handkerchief back in his pocket and slithers down on the far side of the embankment. The others listen nervously.

Peter So much for there not being any Germans out there.

Bobby Those trenches were deserted this morning, they really were. Either they've crept back into them or, most likely, there's some wounded bloke sitting in a shell-hole somewhere with nothing better to do than pick off any British soldier he can find.

Peter Christ, I hope they don't shoot him. He must be bloody mad.

David reappears over the parapet, hauling Sammy with him. There are a few tense moments while he climbs onto the top, but no shots are fired. The others reach up and lift Sammy carefully down from the parapet. He is sweating profusely and is wounded in the chest; he is only just conscious. David climbs down into the trench.

Bobby I'll go and get stretcher-bearers.

He is about to dash off but David gives him a knowing look, his eyes full of pain, and slowly shakes his head. Bobby stops in his tracks and his body goes heavy with despair.

David *(soothingly, to Sammy)* Come on, old top.

He settles down against the firestep and takes Sammy in his arms.

David Get me a blanket. Wrap him up.

Peter and Clem scuttle to find a blanket, which they carefully arrange around Sammy.

David Water. Cloth.

Bobby goes off to fetch them. David gently leans Sammy's head against his shoulder and strokes his hair. Sammy struggles to look up at him, his face suddenly more alert. He is slightly short of breath and finds it difficult to speak.

Sammy What's happening to me?

David *(gently)* You've copped a bit of stick from the Boche, old man. There's nothing for you to worry about.

Sammy It bloody hurts.

David I know it does, Sammy, I know. I can give you something for it.

*He carefully rummages in his pocket for his first field dressing and takes out a tablet of morphia. He gives **Peter** and **Clem** a glance to indicate that they should do likewise, which they do. **David** takes all three morphia pills and gently pushes them under **Sammy**'s tongue.*

David Just leave those there for a minute and you'll be all right. Good man.

Bobby *comes back with a rag and a steel helmet filled with water which he gives to **David**. **David** dips the rag in the water and gently wipes the sweat from **Sammy**'s face.*

Sammy I haven't done a very good job for my King and Country after all, have I?

David We're not fighting for King and Country, Sam, we're fighting for each other. Don't ever forget that.

Sammy But I thought –

David It doesn't matter, old top. It doesn't matter. Keep smiling, eh?

Sammy Yeah.

*A fleeting smile passes over his face, then he looks up at **David** with a bright, concerned expression.*

Sammy I'm sorry, David.

David What about? You've nothing to be sorry for.

Sammy *(weakly)* I'm sorry.

*He buries his face against **David**'s shoulder. **David** holds on to him intensely for several moments as if trying to stop the life escaping from **Sammy**'s body. Gradually he realises it's too late and his face screws up with pain.*

David I've lost him, Bobby.

Bobby We all have.

David   I truly believe in the power of humour and good cheer to fend off the worst of the bombs and bullets, but this – this is like a knife-thrust in the soul.

Bobby   Don't take it hard, David. You can't afford to.

David   It shouldn't have been him. It shouldn't have been him. What prize in war is ever worth the life of a boy of nineteen?

Clem   Seventeen.

David   What?

Clem   Sammy was only seventeen. He joined up underage. He was fifteen when he came out here. He made me promise not to tell anyone that.

David   Oh Clem. I wish I could stop this ridiculous war, its ripples of pain spreading ever outwards through time and space. They tell us to fight for the pride of our nation, the honour of our king, the splendour of battle. Is there such a thing as splendour in battle? Does the nation deserve to be proud? Is there any honour in the status of a king who buys this wretched splendour with the lives of children?

He is finally overcome with emotion. The lights fade down slowly.

ACT TWO, SCENE THREE

*The same scene, a few days later, at night. It is quiet apart from the occasional crash of a falling shell. **Bobby**, **Clem** and **Peter** are huddled around a brazier playing a card game. Its soft red light gives the scene an atmosphere of tranquillity.*

Clem *(putting down a card)* Peter?

Peter What?

Clem How many Germans can you kill with one Mills bomb?

Peter Oh I don't know. About six. Given a fine day and a good concentration of Germans. Four if they're not so well bunched up. Why?

Clem I just wondered.

Peter Now don't start feeling guilty about doing that pill-box. They would only have shot us if we hadn't bombed them out.

Clem Yeah, I know. Your turn, Sarge.

Bobby Sorry. *(he puts down a card)*

Peter Why so preoccupied? You're not getting conscience pangs as well, are you?

Bobby I was just thinking. I killed a German boy once. He can't have been more than about seventeen or eighteen.

Peter Don't even think about it. We've all done it, like it or not. This is no place for conchies.

Clem Y'know, I don't reckon David has ever killed anyone.

Peter I don't know about that. He gave Sammy a morphine overdose. And he knew what he was doing, too.

Bobby Peter! Sammy was dying. The morphine made it bearable, that's all.

Clem I've never seen David use his revolver. Have you?

Bobby No. But an officer's job is to command his men. Not much point in having a pack of dogs and doing the barking yourself. He carries his revolver with him, and he'd use it in self-defence, same as anybody else.

Peter What do aces count as?

Clem   Heroes.

Peter   *(taking a swipe at him)* I don't mean that sort of ace, you silly ass.

Clem   Aces high.

Bobby   Aces low.

Peter   Does anybody know the rules of this game?

Clem   No.

Bobby   No.

Peter   Oh. *(he puts down another card)*

Clem   No rules. No winner.

David enters, holding a small handful of letters and postcards.

David   All right, what joker thought up this one?

They all look up at him innocently. He holds up an army biscuit with a postage stamp attached to it.

David   Writing home on the back of an army biscuit. Clem?

Clem   I'm sorry. We ran out of paper.

David   We're also running out of food. Your A.B. rations are for eating, not writing on.

Clem   I can't eat them, my teeth just squeak on the surface of the damned things, they're so hard. I wanted to see if it would get back to England in one piece.

David   Oh it will, Clem, it will. *(he grins)* I sent one to my best girl last Christmas. If that's all the post for tonight I'd best be off out. The engineers have got a particularly nice mine sap that they want me to have a grovel around in. I'd hate to disappoint them.

Bobby   There's just one thing. Something I didn't tell you about when I came back in off patrol the other morning. I found this, out on the battlefield.

*He takes something from his pocket and holds it out for **David** to see. It is a set of rosary beads.*

David   Conor's rosary. Where did you find it?

Bobby   Just lying in the mud, not far from the other side of our wire. He must have dropped it when we went over the top.

David   Oh Bobby.

Bobby I was going to keep it, just as a kind of memento, but – I think he'd prefer you to have it.

David That's most decent of you. I'm very grateful. *(he takes the rosary)*

Bobby It might come in useful, if you're going crawling about down mine saps.

David Oh, I'll be all right. The only thing I'm worried about is how I'm going to launder my breeches after squelching about knee-deep in Flanders porridge.

Clem David, can I ask you a personal question?

David Fire away. If you'll excuse the unfortunate turn of phrase.

Clem Have you ever killed anyone?

David gives him a sly glance, chuckles knowingly and goes out.

Peter I'm sure that walking-cane of his is some kind of portable howitzer.

Bobby You could be right. Stranger things have happened. Whose go is it?

Clem Oh I don't know. I'm absolutely starving, I wish they'd hurry up and get the ration cart up here.

Peter Mm, me too. Does anybody fancy any trench pudding?

Clem Oh, go on then. Better than nothing.

Peter You'll have to give me your hardtack biscuits then. If you've got any left that you haven't written on.

Clem I've got dozens of the bloody things.

They all collect up their stocks of army biscuits. Peter finds an empty sandbag and they throw the biscuits into it. He ties a knot in the bag to seal it, puts it down on a convenient surface and beats it violently with the handle of an entrenching tool.

Clem *(hardly audible over the racket)* Sarge, do you reckon there's going to be another big show up here?

Bobby Bound to be. It's only because we're holding on to Wipers that the Kaiser can't take Calais. As soon as this lot falls he'll be straight on to the French coast and then there'll be nothing to stop him attacking the British mainland. That's why the Germans want this place so desperately.

Clem Then we're going to need more men, aren't we?

73

Bobby Oh, we'll get more men now. No doubt about it. They're bound to take us out of the line – *(to **Peter**)* shut up you noisy bastard! – they're bound to take us out of the line in the next few days anyway, and send up a new draft to replace the casualties.

Clem I hope you're right. Peter, I do think those A.B.s are suitably pulverised by now.

Peter Just making sure.

Peter throws down the entrenching tool, unties the sack and tips the crumbs into a billycan. He pours in some water from his water-bottle and adds a rather unsavoury-looking dollop of jam from a nearby tin. Then he dangles the billycan in the brazier and stirs the mixture with a bayonet.

Clem He's such a good cook, is our Peter.

Peter My mother works in the kitchens at the local boarding school. She's taught me well.

David re-enters, looking cheerful but a little uncomfortable. He is holding his trench-coat around himself protectively. The others are a little surprised to see him.

Clem That was quick. Have the Royal Engineers got fed up with you already?

David Didn't get that far, old chap. I've brought back a little present from Uncle Boche, that's all. *(he pulls the lapel of his trench-coat aside and reveals a wound in his shoulder)* Splinter from a five-nine. Lucky it didn't take my bally head off, to be honest.

Peter *(horrified)* Christ almighty.

Bobby Come on, we need to get you down to the dressing-station quickly.

David Oh don't fuss. It's only a blighty.

Bobby You still ought to have it seen to. That splinter's got to come out.

David I'm all right. Tough as old boots, me. Now, you're going to have to listen very carefully to this, all of you, because if the medico packs me off home you're going to have to look after yourselves for a bit. There's going to be another assault on Caterpillar Farm. And yes, I know we're more or less back to square one with regard to clearing out those Boche trenches, but those jolly chaps in the R.E.s have dug a nice big tunnel underneath the main German machine-gun post and packed it with 24,000 lbs of ammonal. When that little lot goes up, probably at dawn on Thursday, every Fritz within shooting distance will be blasted to kingdom come and you should find you've got a fairly clear run through the German line. Here, I'll show you. *(he maps the battle plan out on the floor by walking it through and indicating the positions with the end of his walking-cane)* The first thing you'll have to do is run like billy-o across this bit and make your way through what's left of the Boche line, which should by then be a dirty great hole round about here, and then bear off to your left a little way where you'll see the remains of the farm buildings over behind the –

He suddenly collapses on the floor in a cold faint. The others rush over to him and pick him up. Clem has had about as much as he can take and begins to sob a little hysterically. David gradually regains consciousness and gives Clem a bemused look.

David   There's no need for that, Clem. No need at all. We want Wipers not weepers.

Bobby   David, I really think that wound is a bit more serious than you think.

David   Nothing to worry about. Old soldiers never die, and believe me, this one isn't even going to fade away. Just give me a hand down to the dressing-station, there's a good chap.

Bobby hoists David's arm around his shoulders and pulls him to his feet. He is rather unsteady but just about able to walk.

Peter   Can you manage?

Bobby   Yes. He'll be all right. Come on David, just take it steady.

David goes slowly out, heavily supported by Bobby. Clem makes an effort to regain his composure, a little embarrassed about having lost it in the first place.

Peter   Don't worry, Clem. He'll be fine. He's in good hands.

Clem   I know. I just had a bit of a panic. I've seen too many of my friends go west recently. When I saw him go down like that –

Peter   He's lost a bit of blood. It was bound to make him go dizzy. It's only a small wound. Best thing that could happen to a chap, really. I only wish I could get one.

Clem   Yeah, I know what you mean.

Peter   He'll spend the next month or two in a nice cosy hospital back in Blighty, keeping all the nurses amused and annoying all the other officers. He'll get disgustingly fat on decent food and all the chocolate bars the VADs will keep smuggling in for him. And he'll be a very long way away from these blasted guns.

Clem   He's an incredible chap, is David.

Peter   One in a million. Takes a bit of talent, keeping morale up out here.

Clem   Laughing and joking with people while they get blown to bits.

Peter   Yes. In that bloody attack the other day, I was running along with Conor and the machine-guns were rattling around all over the shop and there was nowhere to go for cover, just bodies everywhere and explosions going up left right and centre. And I turned round, and there was David hurtling alongside us, grinning all over his face, and he shouted out 'chins up, chaps!' as he ran past. We gave him a cheery wave, and the next minute Conor was sliced apart by machine-gun fire. Sounds awful, I know, but quite honestly I can't think of any better way to go than to be shoulder to shoulder with your friends and to have a smile on your face. I've kind of got used to the idea of dying young anyway, so it didn't bother me much either way. I remember falling flat on my face in the mud, knowing that I'd been hit and not having any idea whether I was dead or dying or what, and actually laughing. For the first and only time in my life I found I didn't have any worries about death. None whatsoever. Whether I ever got up again or whether I didn't, all that mattered was that I'd had my friends with me and shared that moment with them.

Clem   Christ.

Peter   *(afraid that Clem is going to get emotional again)* Anyway, let's talk about something else for a change. I reckon that trench pudding must be about done by now. *(he retrieves the billycan from the brazier and stirs it around)* Yep. Done to a turn.

*Clem fetches a couple of enamel plates, and **Peter** slops out the contents of the billycan. They are so engrossed in the delighted anticipation of their unappetising meal that they don't notice **Bobby**'s presence behind them. He comes quietly forward and picks up **David**'s walking-cane, which is still lying on the floor where **David** dropped it, and gazes at it with a morose expression.*

Clem   Yum, that looks good.

Peter   *(giggling)* Just like mum's home-made. Wants a bit more salt on it, I reckon.

Clem licks a scrap of the 'pudding' off the end of his finger and suddenly catches sight of Bobby. He freezes. Peter sees the look on Clem's face and turns round. They both stare at Bobby in silence for several moments.

Bobby   David is dead.

Silence.

Peter   You're joking.

Clem   He's not joking.

Peter   What happened?

Bobby   I got him as far as the reserve line. He collapsed again. Just fainted, out like a light. There was a medical orderly nearby and he came over and had a look. He said it was impossible to tell in the dark exactly what the matter was but he thought the shell splinter had gone in further than it appeared, maybe even gone into his heart. At any rate he didn't have a chance to do anything. David was dead. Just like that.

Clem   *(trying not to lose his composure)* But he can't just drop dead. He can't.

Bobby   Clem. He just did. As they say, c'est la guerre.

Clem   But what will we do now?

Peter   Don't get miserable. He'd never forgive us for being miserable.

Clem   We'll never survive without him.

Peter   Clem, we all loved him. If anything he ever said or did means anything to us we have to survive and carry his light for him.

Bobby   Peter's right. We've got to hold on to that and try to make other people understand it too. That way wars like this will never be allowed to happen again.

Clem   Where is he now? I mean, where did you leave him?

Bobby   I left him with the medical orderly. They'll bury him. At least he'll get a proper grave, not like most of the chaps. Something his family can come out and visit after the war.

Clem   We ought to pay some kind of tribute to him though.

Bobby We are. Every moment that we're alive.

Peter *(slapping **Clem** affectionately)* Chin up! *(**Clem** manages a smile)*

Bobby There's something else I've got to do. He once asked me if I'd send a message to his girl for him if he ever got killed.

Peter Did he tell you what to say?

Bobby 'Pip pip old fruit.'

Peter Is that all?

Bobby That's all.

Peter But we haven't got any paper.

Clem We've got some army biscuits though. I've got loads of them in my pack. You can write it on one of those and send it to her.

Bobby Yes, that would appeal to his sense of humour.

*Clem takes a biscuit and a stub of pencil from his pack and hands them to **Bobby**, who writes as carefully and neatly as the biscuit's surface will allow. The others sit in respectful silence, and presently **Clem** begins to sing the hymn 'Abide With Me', very soft and low. The other two join in.*

> Abide with me, fast falls the even tide
> The darkness deepens, Lord with me abide
> When other helpers fail and comforts flee
> Help of the helpless, O abide with me.
>
> Swift to its close ebbs out life's little day
> Earth's joys grow dim, its glories pass away
> Change and decay in all around I see
> O thou who changest not, abide with me.
>
> Hold thou thy cross before my closing eyes
> Shine through the gloom, and point me to the skies
> Heaven's morning breaks, and earth's vain shadows flee –

As they sing the third line there is a brief whining sound followed by a very loud explosion. The singing stops.

Blackout.